A BOY'S BOOK
OF NERVOUS
BREAKDOWNS

YELLOW SHOE FICTION

MICHAEL GRIFFITH, *Series Editor*

A BOY'S BOOK OF NERVOUS BREAKDOWNS

STORIES

TOM PAINE

LOUISIANA STATE UNIVERSITY PRESS

BATON ROUGE

Published with the assistance of the Borne Fund

Published by Louisiana State University Press
Copyright © 2015 by Louisiana State University Press
All rights reserved
Manufactured in the United States of America
LSU Press Paperback Original
First printing

DESIGNER: Mandy McDonald Scallan
TYPEFACE: Whitman

Library of Congress Cataloging-in-Publication Data

Paine, Tom.
 [Short stories. Selections]
 A boy's book of nervous breakdowns : stories / Tom Paine.
  pages ; cm. — (Yellow shoe fiction)
 ISBN 978-0-8071-6124-1 (cloth : alk. paper) — ISBN 978-0-8071-6125-8 (pdf) — ISBN 978-0-8071-
6126-5 (epub) — ISBN 978-0-8071-6127-2 (mobi)
 I. Title.
 PS3566.A342A6 2015
 813'.54—dc23

                                                                                  2015012005

Stories originally appeared in the following periodicals, to whose editors grateful acknowledgment is made: *One Story:* "Marlinspike." *Joyland Magazine:* "Fukushima Mon" and "Hotel Palestine." *Glimmer Train:* "Bagram." *Five Chapters:* "The Southern Strategy." *Zoetrope:* "The Hot War." *World Literature Today:* "Oppenheimer Beach." *Failbetter:* "The Black Box." *Cincinnati Review:* "It Was Just Swimming."

Selections from lyrics in "Fukushima Mon" adapted from translations in *Babylon East: Performing, Dancehall, Roots Reggae and Rastafari in Japan* by Marvin Sterling (Duke University Press, 2010).

For EDC
Amantes Sunt Amantes

CONTENTS

A BOY'S BOOK
OF NERVOUS
BREAKDOWNS

MARLINSPIKE

The blue ferry carrying Julia nodded through the waves to Cyril E. King Airport on St. Thomas. Phineas sat under a tamarind tree above Cruz Bay in his tuxedo, watching it go. The five layers of wedding cake perched in his lap.

He decided to take the cake back to the Westin. He hitched a ride and sat in the back of the Suzuki with the cake on his thighs. The driver, a young Rasta named Desmond, smoked a sugar-sweet bone. Phineas flipped the erect plastic couple at a hiker and laid his palm in the frosted names when the Jeep took air at Power Boyd.

Phineas taught scuba diving at the Westin, with a sideline of shark diving off the North Drop. The crashing of shark populations worldwide kept him up at night. Sometimes he counted jellyfish to put himself to sleep. The cake had been a surprise for Julia. In the last month, he had secretly learned to bake in the kitchen of the hotel. She had spent the morning shopping and sightseeing on St. Thomas with her six bridesmaids. He had met her on the dock with the cake held gloriously overhead, so she could see it over the hundreds of disembarking passengers. He thought the tux a nice theatrical touch.

She got on the next ferry back to St. Thomas with her bridesmaids.

Phineas climbed out of the Jeep and carried the cake through the marble lobby. A giant glob of frosting on his tux looked like a carnation. A young girl in a cowboy hat checking into the Westin with her father tracked him from atop a covey of suitcases, then followed him at a distance, down a hundred marble stairs, past the star pool and waterfall, to the crowded beach.

He raised the cake overhead.

The general manager marched toward Phineas, eyeing the cake. "You're not," he said, "throwing that at the guests?" He was panting and showed all of his teeth.

"I am taking this cake," said Phineas. "And will feed it to the sharks."

"You're angry," said the general manager.

"What tipped you off?"

The manager left to help a guest open an umbrella. Phineas was standing there with the cake high overhead when he felt a light tap on his back.

It was the girl in the cowboy hat.

"I'm a shark," said the girl.

☞ ☜

Phineas took Desmond to the wedding reception that night at Caneel Bay.

His father and mother had flown a lot of Wall Street people down from Westchester, and they were going to throw an island party, wedding or not.

Phineas's sister, Felicia, in from Telluride, found him at the punch. She said she'd been texting with Julia about this decision. She hated to say it, Felicia said, but Julia had a point.

"What?" said Phineas.

"You can do everything," Felicia said. "But your heart's in nothing." Her vocal cords had polyps, and she sounded like Katharine Hepburn. Julia had to do what was good for Julia, Felicia said. Was it going to make Phineas reconsider fantasy island? Would he go back to medical school?

He took the mike from the reggae band and said, to clarify, Julia was still the one. He said his family didn't understand a marriage that wasn't a merger. He said he was sorry his older brother, Angus, couldn't be there, but he'd jumped off the Newport Bridge a few years ago. Phineas said if anyone could explain why Julia got on the ferry that morning after seeing the cake, he was all ears.

Felicia yanked at the mike cord. Then she shoved him into the bass player. Desmond jumped on stage and kissed Felicia, and everyone clapped. Later, Felicia and Desmond had sex under the ferry dock.

At dawn, Phineas broke a beer bottle and etched the letter *J* into his shoulder with a shard of glass.

☞ ☜

Lying by the star pool of the Westin the next night, Phineas saw the little shark girl at the bar. Her cowboy hat made it hard to see her eyes. The girl was alone. The pool was electric green with the underwater lights. She had a single ponytail of red hair to her waist and a terrific sunburn.

His head back, he closed his eyes.

A voice said, "Any more cake?"

"No," said Phineas. "There is only one cake in life."

He guessed she was ten.

"You made the cake?" she said.

"I made the cake."

"Want to make another?"

The next morning, he met the shark girl at the Westin's pastry kitchen, and she ate three éclairs, and they both put red aprons on. It was a ball gown on her. She was all tendons and thin limbs. Claude, the chief pastry chef, set them up and tried to remove her cowboy hat. She slapped his stomach. "Elle est un jeune tigre," Claude said with a laugh. Phineas thought she'd grow bored. Hours passed. They sprinkled flour on each other. Phineas hadn't asked her name.

"Julia," said the girl.

Phineas wept into the mixing bowl.

Julia fixed him with an angry stare.

Her father was a widowed eye surgeon from Savannah. He was here to lead a conference on endoscopic surgery. Julia told Phineas to bend down, and she pushed her pinky up his nostril and scratched at his septum.

"He goes up your nose to get behind your eyeball," she said with a shrug.

"That's impressive."

"You can make wedding cakes."

Julia took to her father the news that Phineas was a scuba instructor and begged him to hire Phineas to teach her to dive. He liked that Phineas had gone to Princeton too, and that they had the same organic chemistry professor. In the lobby, during a break between seminars, Phineas told him about Julia and the wedding. He shook his head, somber, but then insisted on calling Professor Kinkaid—with whom he kept in touch—to tell him about meeting Phineas. As Julia yanked Phineas away by the hand, her father was laughing into his cell phone: "No, no, he's not a doctor. He swims with sharks. He's going to teach my daughter to scuba dive."

Phineas and Julia swam out to the mouth of Great Cruz Bay with masks and snorkels. Julia liked to barrel roll. She rode Phineas's shoulders down to the reef, chased parrotfish, and examined bubbles erupting like a string of tiny pearls from the sand. A five-foot barracuda lolled past, and the two followed until its black barcode darkened in warning. It pivoted back to them, toothed jaws yawning. They ended up on the giant orange castle float anchored off the beach. They did full twists off the twelve-foot tower before hitting the water crying, "I hate wedding cake!" Their aprons looked like bloodstains on the beach.

When they swam ashore, Phineas told Julia to sit very still, and he dribbled wet sand on her head, then added a circlet of little pink shells. "How does my crown look?" she said. "Can we lock it in the hotel safe tonight?" Phineas grabbed a long Westin towel off a guest chair and placed it on her shoulders. She carefully stood and walked like a queen down the beach. Phineas followed, holding her train up. Guests on shaded lounge chairs gazed at them with small smiles.

Sometimes Julia reached into her backpack and texted her father. "He's hiding in his eyeballs," she said. "He can't help it since my mother got thrown."

Julia invited Phineas to dinner. It was odd, but Phineas decided to go with it. She took him to Aqua Tonic, the most expensive of the three restaurants at the Westin. Her father met with doctors in small groups in the evening and then went to Cruz Bay to drink. He gets plastered on scotch, Julia added, rolling her eyes. A woman with a red frangipani blossom in her white hair stopped by the table and said, "Your daughter looks like that little movie star." She tried to put the blossom in Julia's hair, but Julia clutched her cowboy hat.

Phineas put the blossom atop his newly shaved head.

Julia waved her room key and insisted Phineas order an expensive bottle of wine. He hesitated before ordering. When the sommelier left, she used a straw to add drops into her water glass until it tinted rose.

"Make a toast," said Julia, holding up her glass.

Phineas wept.

Julia stared at him.

He walked out of the restaurant with the blossom still floating on his head. He pretended he didn't know what Julia was laughing about, and when it tumbled, he said, "It's raining flowers!"

Julia texted her father. He was in Cruz Bay at dinner with some doctors talking eyeballs. Julia said on the way down he forgot her in the Charlotte airport. American Airlines put her on the next flight to St. Thomas with a badge. Phineas and Julia walked at dusk along the shore and climbed inside a beached wooden yacht. The stern had been chiseled off by Hurricane Marilyn. Phineas found a water-plumped copy of *Wind, Sand and Stars* by Antoine de Saint-Exupéry. Julia found a marlinspike under the mahogany floorboards, and Phineas explained it was a tool sailors used to open the most impossible knots.

Julia said her father hated eyeballs.

The two sat on the warm deck of the wreck. Phineas tied knots in a few feet of blue bowline. Julia wiggled them open with her marlinspike. Phineas banged on the hull with his fist and said she was built like a bank vault. The two discovered some driftwood and played the hull like a giant drum. Julia insisted Phineas learn carpentry and sail somewhere.

The yacht's name was *Mandrake*. She was up from Trinidad. Phineas said sailors could once read the sea as if it were a novel, every ripple a sentence. The moon slid up like a thief, and St. Thomas floated in a brushstroke of clouds.

Phineas talked. When he was ten, he loved a girl named Katie Davis and took a bus across town to stand in front of her house: 514 New Meadow Road, New Britain, Connecticut. The police hauled him home, and he kicked the seat until they handcuffed him. He put his poems in her yellow Keds at gym, stole a shirt from her locker and slept with it over his pillow. She went to the senior prom with Harry Haggerty and was now a famous shoe designer who lived in a large loft in Chelsea with a geneticist who liked hip-hop.

He carried Julia on his shoulders back to the hotel. They made a giant moon shadow on the beach. After Julia went to bed, Phineas sat in the hall with his back to her door. She had her own room, and her father stumbled home near dawn. He leaned against the wall. Julia had put her cowboy hat on Phineas's head.

Her father said, "That's her mother's cowboy hat."

"I wondered."

"It wasn't an affectation," said Julia's father. "Her mother was a rodeo queen. And a barrel racer. She was thrown by her horse last year in Montana. See if you can get Julia to talk. I'll pay you for your time."

Phineas didn't sleep. He sat through a morning shower in a beach chair by the star pool and swam furiously out to sea for the sunrise. He wished he hadn't made the wedding cake. He wished he didn't want to climb palm trees all the fucking time. For a few moments his raised arms and his hands were copper. He watched the first ferry arrive from St. Thomas and tried to sink out of sight. He could hear the blind throb of the engine, and he covered his ears. That throb was locked inside him now and swam ashore with him.

Julia was standing on the beach.

"My father said you can drive his Jeep today," said Julia. "He's sick and staying in bed. Another doctor is going to give the eyeball talks."

Julia handed him the silver key, and he handed over her cowboy hat, which he had wrapped in a towel and hidden behind some giant aloe vera. The roosters crowed up in Power Boyd.

He took her to the ruins of the America Hill plantation. As they walked up the trail past the giant raised tombs of the Danish owners, a swarm of jack spaniel wasps stung Julia. Phineas took her arm and sucked the welts. He carried her on his shoulders the rest of the way. She ran her fingers meditatively over the bristle on his cheeks.

"You're tough," said Phineas. "There were nine stings. Jack spaniels are nasty."

"I never cry."

Phineas placed his palms on the ocher stones of the plantation house ruins. Once he had wanted to be an architect. He had dreams of houses made of water. He traced the rough cement with his fingers. Trees grew out of the tops of the tumbling walls, and strangler vines reached up like hands and yanked down whole trees. They stood in the shadows of the dank walls and looked at Jost Van Dyke across the water.

"I want to go," said Julia.

Julia's arm was swollen. He wrapped it in a poultice of noni tree leaves he warmed in tea water at the Westin and sat with her on the beach. As he resoaked and reapplied the leaves, Phineas told her the story of the Ashanti prince sold into bondage on St. John who led the first slave rebellion in the Western Hemisphere.

"What happened to him?" said Julia.

"He jumped off Ram's Head rather than surrender."

"We'd jump too," said Julia. "Right?"

That night Phineas slept outside his tent on the rocky shore of Johnson's Bay and let the mosquitoes feast on him. In a dream Katie Davis pointed to her heart, and it was swarming with jack spaniels. He put his lips to the warm, pulsing hole and sucked. He awoke from a dream he was running down the beach with a mouth full of blood.

☞ ☜

Topless Tina kicked him awake and offered to take him sailing to Jost Van Dyke on her gaff-rigged schooner, *Annie Bonnie*. She was a liveaboard sailor who moored in the turtle grass of Johnson's Bay.

"Can I bring Julia?" said Phineas.

Julia wore her marlinspike on some lanyard line, her cowboy hat, and a black-and-white polka-dotted bikini. Phineas brought a case of Heineken and the book he and Julia had found in the wreck of the *Mandrake*.

When they climbed aboard, Tina flicked the top off a Heineken with Julia's marlinspike and with one arm yanked her Bolongo Bay T-shirt over her head.

Phineas tried not to look at her famous breasts.

Topless Tina told Julia that on the *Annie Bonnie*, piratical girls went topless.

Julia asked if Tina had any impossible knots.

Saint-Exupéry wrote, "It comes over us that we shall never again hear the laughter of our friend, that this one garden is forever locked against us. And at that moment begins our true mourning."

They were gunnel down with a 20-knot breeze near Ram's Head on the return to St. John. Julia was in the bowsprit tied by a safety line, riding the plummets of the giant rollers, when a gust ripped the cowboy hat from her head and into their spangled moonlit wake. Phineas held Julia in a bear hug as she struggled for the stern. She punched his face and bit his arm, and he had no doubt she was willing to jump.

☞ ☜

Phineas took Julia to Kiddel Bay. It wasn't sandy, so there were no tourists. He had scuba gear in case she wanted to try diving in shallow water.

In the dirt parking lot was an old tamarind tree with a tire swing. Phineas said he knew how to make tamarinds into jam. Julia emptied her mesh snorkel bag and gathered hundreds. They sat in gravel and organized the tamarinds into a circle. Julia developed a ranking of tartness based on color and nibbled on so many she got a stomachache.

Walking in the rocky shallows, they found half an eel.

"Barracuda," said Phineas.

The next day, St. Patrick's Day, Phineas borrowed a bike, and they decorated it in green bunting. Topless Tina painted shamrocks on her cheeks, and she rode in the "World's Shortest Parade" from the tennis courts to The Quiet Mon Pub.

They sat across from the international ferry dock. A man yelling he had lost his passport was forced back onto the Tortola ferry. People laughed as the loud diesel roared and drowned the man's pleadings. Julia speared her French fries with the marlinspike, and they played dominoes. She cracked the dominoes hard on the table like the West Indian men. Two other ferries blasted their horns and left the over-crowded harbor. Desmond, the Rasta who had given Phineas a ride with the wedding cake, was selling coconuts on the beach. Phineas bought one for Julia.

Desmond sat with them while Julia drank the coconut milk from a straw and then, holding it in his callused palm, chopped it open with his machete. He gave Julia chunks of the white flesh, and she ate ravenously.

"I want to climb a coconut tree," said Julia to Desmond.

"She said I'd be climbing coconut trees forever," said Phineas to Desmond.

Desmond shook his head. "I'm sorry, mon."

"You really want to climb a coconut tree, Julia?"

"Yes. Don't you?"

☞ ☜

Phineas headed up Bordeaux Mountain in the Jeep. Julia finally asked if there were coconut trees on the mountain, and Phineas said nothing. Julia glanced at him as she took apart her braid with the marlinspike.

There was a long descent on the other side of the mountain to Coral Bay. They drove through a squall in the open Jeep and then stopped for two iguanas fighting in the road.

Phineas parked at Salt Pond and took Julia's hand. He walked her down to the empty beach and then along the shore. Soon they were on a rocky cactus trail and frightened a goat. It clattered in behind them later and butted Julia from behind. She rubbed its head, and it chewed on her hair. It was an hour's uphill climb. When the sun went down, they sat on a rock in the dark and waited for the moon. In the dark they could hear the crashing surf. Under the enormous yellow moon, the two walked higher. Bats swam around them.

They came to a high rocky plateau and stood under the stars on the bluff over the sea. A blustery wind arose, and Phineas pulled Julia in tight against him.

"Is this Ram's Head?" said Julia.

Phineas nodded.

"Where the prince jumped?" said Julia.

Phineas nodded.

The sea was confused, crashing on the cliffs below.

☞ ☜

Phineas drove back up over Bordeaux through clouds and down the serpentine road to Cruz Bay. They picked up two hikers from Australia at the head of the Reef Bay Trail. One of them let Julia wear his strong headlamp and when he hopped out of the Jeep told her to keep it. She blinded Phineas when she looked at him.

"Can we find a coconut tree now?" Julia said.

He walked with her along Cruz Bay beach. Julia stared at her feet in the water lit by her new headlamp. She said she was taking the ferry away in the morning.

There were three coconut trees near the Beach Bar. Topless Tina was sitting under one of them with Desmond smoking a bone.

The boats in the harbor bobbed together from the wake of the ferry. One of the yachts still had Christmas lights blinking up the mast. The band was playing "Danny Boy," and tourists were dancing a drunken jig in the sand. The yellow moon was rolling over St. Thomas.

Julia jumped up on a plastic chair next to Tina and wrapped her arms around a palm tree. She put her cheek to the tree with her eyes closed and then wriggled upward a half dozen feet. She clung there with her eyes squeezed shut, hugging the tree. Her red hair hung loose to her waist.

A gust rippled across the black water of the bay.

Phineas sat down next to Topless Tina and took a hit off the bone.

"I want your cock," Topless Tina whispered to Phineas.

"What's a cock?" said Julia from the palm tree.

"A male rooster," said Topless Tina.

"Does Phineas have a cock?"

"Is she messing with me?" whispered Tina.

"Julia, are you messing with Tina?"

"I'm a pirate," said Julia.

"She's messing with you."

Desmond told Julia to come down from the tree. Phineas thought he was worried. But Desmond slid his leather belt out of the loops in his ragged black pants. He handed the belt to Julia and showed her how to wrap it around the tree and cinch herself loosely.

She leaned back against the belt, her thin legs clenching the tree.

"Take my marlinspike," she said to Phineas.

She went up the tree like a spider monkey.

"That girl a true island girl," said Desmond.

The three adults sat under the palm. Phineas went to the bar and brought back Heinekens and two shots of Jager. He sat with the marlinspike in his lap, sipping the beer and looking at Julia twenty feet up the tree. He knew she was looking down when the headlamp flashed in his eyes. Phineas squeezed the marlinspike in his hand, pressed the tip into his palm until he saw a bead of blood.

Then Julia was up near the fronds and coconuts. She was at least thirty feet up. He stood and called for her to come down. The headlamp looked down at him for a long count and then out to sea. Topless Tina called to Julia, and Desmond called out he wanted his belt back.

A few seconds later the belt dropped at their feet in the sand. One of the tourists spotted her up the tree and yelled that she was going to kill herself. Someone said he was calling 911. The band stopped playing, and tourists rushed out of the bar with their drinks and circled the tree. Someone dragged a red tarp from a dinghy on the beach, and five men held it open below the tree like firemen.

Phineas picked up the belt from the sand. He strapped himself to the palm tree, clenched his bare knees to the trunk, and started up. Every once in a while, he saw the light up in the palm fronds glance down at him.

The tourists were quiet, their heads tilted back.

Phineas kissed the top of Julia's head and looked at the stars through the palm fronds. A ferry rumbled out for St. Thomas, disappearing into the dark waters.

FUKUSHIMA MON

Last month, by Gmail, I got the invitation to your funeral in Japan on March 11. It took me a few breaths to remember that was the first anniversary of the 2011 Tohoku earthquake. It would seem impossible to forget—even for the span of a few breaths—one of most the powerful earthquakes ever recorded, or a tsunami 140 feet high. It would seem impossible to forget a force powerful enough to jilt the earth four inches off its axis, or leave us with days that are shorter. And then the meltdown of three of the seven reactors at the Fukushima Daiichi nuclear power plant. Could I forget that for a moment? Or the heroism of your father, Masao, who saved the northern third of Japan?

And then there was you, Himamari.

Could I forget *you?*

That this was your funeral, and not one of the memorials taking place in Iwate Prefecture and Sendai for the fifteen thousand or more killed in the tsunami, and that you were not gone *yet*—yes, that took another couple of deep breaths. It is unusual to be invited to a funeral before there is a death, but as you said, "It is a Alice world now." Knowing about a planned suicide does not mean you don't try to stop it. So I left my ketch *Sunflower* stern-anchored to some mangroves and got on the first of several planes that took me from Jamaica to London to Tokyo. And I brought you a copy of *Alice* with the original illustrations by Tenniel, although I prefer yours. For the last year I have slept with your hand-drawn "Anime Alice" under my pillow, and when I can't

sleep sit on deck under the stars and touch each page with my fingertips, while the boat rocks in Kingston harbor, and I listen to your CD
playing in the cabin belowdeck. Your cover of Judy Mowatt's "I Shall
Sing" makes me hang my head. I keep your *Alice* wrapped in plastic as
much as I can, as the salt air is hard on rice paper.

There are factual things you never knew: in February 2011, a month
before the three-act disaster, I was sent by GE back to Japan to help
upgrade the emergency response at Fukushima Daiichi. Although the
TEPCO (Tokyo Power) report of earlier that year said there was "no
need to take prompt action" about vulnerabilities at the plant, GE knew
if Fukushima had a Three Mile Island, it would hurt the multi-trillion-
dollar nuclear power market for the next fifty years, and they pressured
TEPCO to accept me as a consultant. I had a twenty-year history in
Japan, and first went there after graduating from Brown with a degree
in East Asian studies. It was a pretty good deal: I was hired by the Japanese government in 1992 to teach high school students on Okinawa
to speak English, but mostly I was sent from school to school to stand
around and speak English as a model American, and so I talked about
the Red Sox. After school, I played baseball or basketball with the kids
or windsurfed over coral reefs with Japanese friends. I made $45,000
a year, paid no taxes and had no real expenses, drank sake every night,
and slept on the beach in a hammock.

And then, one day, I dug in the sand.

This was one of the Okinawan beaches where marines came ashore
in World War II, and the white sand I walked on barefoot was, in truth,
soaked with blood. Tanks slouched in the sand, and crumbling concrete fortifications waved rusted rebar like lunatics. One day I moved
the stones of the burial cairn of a Japanese soldier and dug in the sand
until I scraped at a pitted white bone with my fingernails. That night I
ended up in surgery, an emergency appendectomy. The appendix burst
just as the surgeon sliced open my abdomen, and I got a bad case of
peritonitis and almost didn't make it through the night. Then I was
sick for weeks in the hospital. The last week, I was next to a fellow
gaijin with an arrhythmic heart, a guy named Bob McCormick from

North Dakota who worked for GE at Fukushima, and when he heard me speak fluent Japanese with the nurses, he hired me.

And that was how, twenty years later, I was back at Fukushima in the month before the March 11 disasters. Most of the two decades were spent at various Japanese nuclear reactors, because they all were pretty much built with GE parts. I was a workaholic, and never took time out to see Japan, or get married, or have a girlfriend. That last February I worked eighteen-hour days with everyone from firemen to engineers, right up to your father the plant manager, so the plant would be better prepared in the event of, say, a 9.0 earthquake twenty miles away and fifteen miles down that would send a forty-six-foot wall of water crashing over the seawall.

It was on March 9, two days before the earthquake, that your father, Masao, handed me a ticket for the bullet train to Tokyo and booked a week for me at the Ichiban Sheraton. Your father, as you know, loved all things Italian, and had been having me to dinner a couple nights a week. In a lot of ways he wasn't very Japanese, your father. He drank whiskey hard, called out the stupidities of the government, TEPCO, and GE, and overall, was far from a compliant *salariiman*. It was only while stirring a marinara for him that I learned he was *hibakusha*, the child of Nagasaki survivor, and had grown up with all that prejudice against the "contaminated ones." It is strange to think a *hibakusha* would chose to make a career of working with what are really slow-cooking nuclear bombs. It is stranger still to think that if Nagasaki radiation made him an outcast, it was perhaps his *hibakusha* status that molded him into a man able to defy the direct order of the prime minister of Japan, continue to cool with seawater the three reactors melting down and save Japan from an explosion at Fukushima the size of a dozen Nagasakis.

Your father sent me to Tokyo because he knew somehow that after almost twenty years I was tired in my bones from overwork, but also because he had heard me listening to Bob Marley on my iPod one night when we were working in Daiichi Three. We were reinspecting venting pipes for microscopic weld cracks. He tapped me on the shoulder—it was two in the morning—and I jumped a foot, and he thought this hilarious. Then he yanked my earphone out, put it to his ear, and said, "Bob Marley?"

He looked murderous.

He pulled me to his office by the elbow, we drank Jim Beam and talked again about the criminal nineteen-foot seawall, and finally he reached into his brown steel desk and handed me your schoolgirl photo. And then your father's eyes moistened, and he said, "Would you go see her?" It came out over the next hours how your mother, Sachiko, had disappeared when you were three when your father left her family's farm and took his first job at Fukushima Daiichi, and how at fourteen you ran away from home with the lead singer of a local reggae band called Sanshin Nanjaman. He said you were a dancer then, but now, three years later, lead singer in a band called Fukushima Mon. Then he made me answer a question: *Why did Bob Marley come to Japan in 1979?* I didn't know Marley *had*, but then had to listen to your father give a short history of reggae in Japan, from recordings of Marley playing that year, on his first visit, with the band Pecker Power and the Flower Travellin' Band, to Joe Yamanaka and Mute Beat, and the "tinny riddims" of Naoya Matsuoka Minako. He was sure I would have met the Okinawan singers in U-Dou or Platy during my time on that island. Your father knew everything—in his methodical engineer way—about reggae in Japan, but he also despised it, and as he played recording after recording for me, he burned me with kamikaze eyes, and kept drunkenly challenging me (once I thought he was going to punch me) to answer the question: *Why did Bob Marley come to Japan in 1979?*

Then at dawn he slammed the old paint-stained CD player in the bottom drawer of his desk, took out a photo framed with purple wood and metal gold stars, and gently placed it in my lap. He motioned to it with a jabbing gesture and grimaced at the ceiling. The arteries were popping in his thick neck. I looked down at the photo. You were sitting in a garden fenced with sticks at about age five. You were plump, with black bangs that almost covered your pretty eyes, and naked but for a little purple kimono. Someone—was it you?—had made a perfect circle of a hundred tomatoes, and you sat in the center of them, grinning at the camera with your mouth wide open as if you were singing, holding out two of the juiciest red tomatoes to the camera, and then I saw that it wasn't a circle of tomatoes around you, but a heart.

As your father sipped, I studied the photo. The garden was disciplined, but brimming with ingredients for an Italian meal: in addition to hundreds of tomatoes bending the vines, I spotted asparagus, broccoli, eggplant, bell peppers, hot peppers, zucchini, and a neatly stoned-off section of herbs like parsley, oregano, thyme, and basil. (I took my time studying, because your father was weeping.) The background was all farmland, but on the horizon, no bigger than the tomatoes in your little hands, I saw the gray boxes of the Fukushima Daiichi reactors. There were shovels and gloves and wooden baskets, a wheelbarrow, and down in the corner of the foreground, a long knife was plunged into soil that was like chocolate from a fresh tilling.

A few hours later, I was on the bullet train to Tokyo, slicing through the rice fields at 150 kilometers per hour. In a folder on my lap I had directions to the Sheraton in the Mikano district, and to Babylon 666, the club you would be playing that night. Someone had left a paperback on the train—a novel by Mishima—and I tried to read it, but it caused me too much anxiety to be existing, even for a few hours, without the frame of a job. The last time I had read a novel for pleasure was when I windsurfed in Okinawa that year after college.

I dumped my suitcase on the bed in the Sheraton, and yanked shut the curtains, as the light was severe that day. But I yanked the curtain so hard it ripped its little wheels out, and so I just ripped it the rest of the way down, and then stood there with this awful shroud in my arms, looking out over the traffic of a Tokyo workday. Until evening, I lay on the bed and looked down at my Thom McCan dress shoes. Then I got up, took a shower, and lay naked on the bed looking at my reddish toes for a couple more hours. The fact that I had a goal: to find you at your club, Himamari, was a very good thing. I dug in my suitcase and pulled out a sun-bleached T-shirt—a favorite back in my Okinawa days—put on a leather jacket, and headed into the night.

There was a crowd outside the industrial garage doors of Babylon

666, and three naked-to-the-waist bouncers. One of the big guys with an earphone and a Muslim skullcap pulled me forward. I paid the cover and fought my way to the bar, then the empty stage. From my angle, I could see backstage behind the yellow curtains, and spotted you right away. You had the same bangs, and you were the same exuberant child as in your father's photo. But what I recognized most of all was your mouth: You were singing, warming up, and jumping up and down in that springy Rastafarian way, but your open singing mouth was so you. Something about it was so ecstatic.

You took the stage and said: *Ikkyoku me, kore wa Kami no koto.*

You had me from those first words: *This first song is about divine issues.* I've learned a lot about reggae and its sense of the divine in nature since moving to Kingston—you could say I moved to Kingston *for* reggae—but I have never felt as, to put it simply, happy as I did that night, listening to your band Fukushima Mon, crushed so hard against the bandstand by Japanese Rasta-loving teenagers that I had to push back to fill my ribcage with a breath. Every time you stopped bouncing up and down across the stage, threw your arms open like you were rejoicing in sparks thrown down from Bob Marley's big spliff up in heaven, pulled the microphone up to your mouth, every time you sang a note, I got this electric pulse that traveled from the soles of my feet up through my chest and out the top of my head. It was about the middle of your second set that you looked directly at me, and you smiled in a way that was so *gentle* that I mouthed, "I love you." It was not like me at all—in fact it was the first time I had ever said those words to any woman—and I left the front of the stage and tried to hide in the dancing crowd.

I remember this lyric from near the end of your show. You sang:

> Shiki ga irodoru yutaka na color
> Daichi ga umidasu minori no aka
> Wakai ibuki ga hanatsu pawaa wa mugendai

I carved it in English on a mahogany plank I found drifting in Kingston Bay, and now it hangs in the galley of my ketch:

Rich colors of the four seasons
Red of the harvest that the earth bears
The unleashed power of the breath of youth is infinite

As I said, there was a huge crowd, so I was surprised when your long show was over, and everyone was milling around, that you found me at a table in the back.

"I saw you," you said. "Singing in Japanese."

I admitted I had tried to sing along, but stopped because I wanted to hear your voice.

I said your voice made me see rice fields. It was the most poetic thing I could think to say, and I wanted to say the right thing.

You bowed your head. "That is my goal."

"Rice fields?"

"Yes," and then with a smile you added, "Or maybe tomatoes."

You played with your dreads, which were painted gold. "Do you like the gold?" you asked.

I said that no gold would suit you, too.

"Thanks," you said. "I'm thinking of washing it out. I'm more roots reggae than rapper-dancehall."

The guy I took to be your boyfriend or just your bass player was now staring me down from another big table, where he sat with the rest of the band and a lot of groupies. All the girls had some gold in their dreads, and wore Daisy Duke cutoff jeans and knee-high socks.

You sang a few bars of Bob Marley's *Exodus*:

Open your eyes and look within
Are you satisfied with the life you're living?

I was caught looking at the medallion dangling between your breasts. Your white schoolgirl shirt was open, and you had on a purple bra. The gold medallion was as large as my fist, at its center a disk of jade. You took the disk in your two hands and stretched out your long white neck to look down at it with theatrically wide eyes. "My father had it made when I was born. He came from a family of metal craftsmen in Nagasaki. My name means Sunflower." For a long time you looked down at the disk, and then, raising your eyes—and I saw for a second a sadness that scared me—you asked, "Would you help me write a song in English?"

I said I'd help, but that you spoke English very well. I said I wasn't much of a writer, and that if I had any training, it was in systems management.

"Not American English! I want it to sound Jamaican."

You shook your head and sighed deeply.

"I'm working on a song called 'Durty Gul.'"

"Dirty Girl?" I said, and you said, "Dirty. Like the dirt. I love dirt."

I wanted to know more, but your boyfriend/bass player was playfully punching my arm. Then he was less playfully gripping my bicep. "Who da mon dat kill Bob Marley?" he asked suddenly, several times, and flashed a gold tooth.

"Why would he know?" you said, slapping his chest. "Let go, Yoshiki."

He glared at me, but dropped his arm.

"Yoshiki's crazy," you said. "He's sure the CIA killed Bob Marley. And he doesn't like me talking to men, either."

I stood there and looked at Yoshiki, who asked angrily if I knew "Tony Rebel" and then sang: Come, come, come, judgment a come, come, come all the while making an inventory of his dreadlocks, which went to his waist.

Then he dropped his dreads and got in my face and sang:

Minna akogareru no kuni
Nihin ni genbaku otoshita Americka

Which he sang then in English, not trusting my Japanese:

The free country everyone love
This America drop the bomb on Japan

You pushed Yoshiki away from me and said, "We've got to go. I've got to get these guys to practice my new songs," and then you added, "Do you speak Chinese, too? Next year, I plan to take the band to Beijing. They need songs about dirt."

I said I knew just a little Chinese, but told you how much I'd enjoyed your music.

You closed your eyes. "You're the first one," she said. "All the others just want to fuck me." You did a vocal exercise, and I saw your pretty mouth open in that way, as if you were singing the world into existence. "You'd think he'd not send old American men to check on me," she said, touching her white shirt. "They all have a thing about the Asian schoolgirl look."

"You knew all the time?"

You closed your eyes for a moment, then reached out and touched my hand. "Why don't you come to another concert?" you asked. "We play here every Wednesday, and at Bushido's on Saturday night."

I lied and said my trip to Tokyo was about over.

"You have to get back before the plant blows up," you said. You didn't look like you were joking.

Of course, this was the day before, so looking back, well, what can I say, Himamari?

You took the medallion off your chest and kissed it. "It will someday, you know," you said. "I've known it since I was a little girl in Fukushima. I saw it in nightmares that started a few years after my father went to work there. He wasn't supposed to work there. We lived on my mother's family farm in Tomioka, and he was supposed to be a farmer. But he looked at Fukushima Daiichi every day plowing in the field, and it took over his brain. I could see the reactors from my bedroom, and I didn't want that to happen to me, so when I was eight I papered over my window, and from then on, even when I was in the yard, or the garden, or getting in and out of the car, I'd not look over there. I walked around for years with my eyes on the ground, and my father thought I was just being a good Japanese girl."

It seemed for a moment you were in a deep trance, but then you looked at me and said with a small amount of alarm, "You *do* work at Fukushima, right?"

I thought we had established that, but you looked so worried that I reached out and held your arm and said, *yes*.

"Of course," you said nodding. "It shows in your face, and in your hands."

It struck me that this couldn't be true, but I drank my beer and looked at my hands.

"But you like reggae music," you said, as if I was a big question mark.

You stared into my eyes and said, "Sometimes men who worked with my father at the nuclear plant would come after work to our farmhouse. We had a stone path to the front door my mother put in when my parents were first married. It was like a Zen garden. You had to step from stone to stone, or you stepped on dirt. And those nuclear men treated it like a minefield, like if they stepped off the stones they would be blown apart."

You held my eyes for a moment, and then went on: "Just before I left home for good with my boyfriend at fourteen, when I wasn't practicing my music, I liked to work in the garden. I knew I was going to have to run away from my father, and the only things that calmed me were reggae music and having my hands in the dirt. Sometimes my boyfriend would stand there with his guitar and sing to me as I planted and weeded and watered. It made me happy, and the plants liked it too. He was twenty-two, and had been to Jamaica, and had dreads to his shoulder. He thought my father, and anyone who worked at Fukushima, was a true citizen of Babylon, the oppressor, and to be hated. And he talked Jamaican Rasta patois. So my father's co-workers came by, and they would be making their way across the stone steps, and he—his name was Hibikilla—would sing louder and shake his dreads, and they knew he was cursing them. Rastas do not believe the meek shall inherit the earth, but that it is right to stand up to Babylon's injustice, evil, and oppression with the strength of a lion. So he shook his dreads—his lion's mane—at those nuclear engineers, and then finally one day he and my father got in a big fight, and I walked down the road with Hibikilla—we see cars as instruments of Babylon—and so now I am in Tokyo, in exodus from the dirt of my ancestors, but I sing about the dirt of Fukushima, and I know someday I must return there, and place my hands in it again, and grow things again in that dirt."

And with that, you lowered your head.

I ordered another beer and watched as you, and then the rest of your band, got up to leave. Yoshiki stormed out first, spearing his guitar case into the crowd. Kazuhiko followed, waving his drumsticks magically in the air, then you, Himamari, turned back and flapped your medallion at me. It caught the lights and sent a dozen reflections skittering across the black ceiling like fish.

A minute later, you came back into Babylon 666 with Yoshiki. You came up to me looking exasperated, and Yoshiki came right out with it and said, "Who killed Bob Marley?"

A glance at you and I knew to say, "The CIA."

Yoshiki grinned and nodded and put out his fist, and we bumped them several times, and then he pulled me into an embrace and said all was "Irie" between us now. As Yoshiki turned to loudly pronounce to some other Rastas that all was "Irie" with the *gaijin* now, you whispered in my ear, "Tell my father he is to be a grandfather."

I looked at Yoshiki, and you nodded.

And then you were gone.

And early the next morning—five days earlier than planned—I got back on the bullet train, and headed to Fukushima Daiichi. At noon on March 11 I got off at the Fukushima station, and instead of going to work I drove along the coastline, and pulled over at Tomioka. It was a quiet day, but the sea was ashen. And then abruptly trucks raced past, and as I looked down at the harbor I saw fishermen leaping into their boats along the dock. Within minutes, twenty trawlers were heading straight out to sea. This was still an hour before the earthquake. I learned later that animals had been fleeing to high ground all morning. Maybe the fishermen took cue from the animals, otherwise, how did they know? Only three of those fishing boats made it up and over the hundred-mile-an-hour tsunami.

Back at the nuclear plant, it was eerily peaceful, and birds were singing as I headed into Building A. But as I walked toward the main control room, there was an incredible rumble, and I was thrown against the wall. The shaking got stronger and stronger, and as I stumbled in, I saw pipes ripping off the wall. Workers were fleeing all around me, yelling about the coming tsunami. Your father bowed to me formally, and not long after, the tsunami crashed over the seawall and plucked up the five-thousand-ton fuel tanks for the backup diesel generators. Your father and I stood together outside and watched them sink into the sea. We both knew that without the backup generators, when the main power died and there was no way to pump cool water into the reactors, we would have no way to keep the nuclear fuel from melting down.

The control room was dark and silent. Then some of the senior nuclear engineers found a few flashlights. No one was speaking, but I heard a magic marker squeaking on a white board, and a flashlight played over it:

15:42 Emergency
15:48 Loss of power

And the engineer was adding:

16:36 Cooling Systems Shut Down

This last line was the "Chernobyl" line.

A glance at our dosimeters told us, as expected, that radiation levels were rising rapidly: Nuclear meltdown had begun. But we didn't know anything else about what was going on inside the reactors, because without electricity, no gauges were operational. Every engineer in that room knew that not only was he doomed when the reactors blew up, but the northern third of Japan would be uninhabitable for thirty thousand years.

The engineers turned to look at your father. He was silent for a minute, then told the men to run to their cars. I saw a few engineers head toward the doors. But he explained he wanted them to run to their cars and bring back their car batteries. When they did, lugging them in one by one, he used them to power up some of the pressure gauges in Reactor One, and we learned that the overheating rods were turning the last of the cooling water into steam and hydrogen, and that the pressure in the reactor was already in the red zone.

The cardinal rule in nuclear power is: *Never vent into the atmosphere.* But it was either vent this hydrogen and steam—and all the radiation that would escape with it—or wait for the reactor unit to explode. But the vents, too, operated on electricity. And there was no electricity.

Once again, the engineers looked to your father. He grabbed some manuals, motioned to me and two others, and we pored over them by flashlight. And then your father said loudly: "I need a volunteer to go with me."

There was silence.

It was possible to move the vents by hand by turning two steel wheels. But to do so meant entering the reactor core, and that was probably a suicide mission. Your father at this point sent home—if they still had a home or families, with fifteen thousand dead and hundreds of thousands of homes lost—more than 250 workers. Then he asked again for a volunteer. I raised my hand, but he shook his head and said something about "47 Ronin."

I have since read a great deal about the "47 Ronin" and how these forty-seven samurai avenged the death of their lord after two years of careful planning, then committed mass *seppuku* on his grave after showing him the head of his enemy. It is a true story that gets at the heart of bushido, the samurai code of honor.

A few moments later, an engineer by the name of Kazuhiko Kokubo raised his hand. We all watched your father and Kazuhiko put on hazmat suits, and I walked with them as far as the steel door into the reactor.

At 67 millisieverts, your father and Kazuhiko had nine minutes to get to the wheel. It was done, but while in the reactor core, your father took—on top of the general extreme radiation exposure—a *beta* radiation burn when he stepped into a puddle and the water breached the seal on his right boot. He never spoke about this burn.

It was after this that your father led a group of Tokyo firefighters (later called by the media the "Fukushima 50") in placing a pipeline from the ocean into the reactor core. I helped with this operation, and at times we were spied on by American drones flying low overhead. We in turn watched our dosimeters spike wildly, often into the deadly thousand-millisievert zone. Your father dragged the final length of fire hose into the actual reactor core. It was the placing of this hose—which poured seawater around the overheating nuclear rods—that kept the reactor from exploding like ten Chernobyls. The use of this pipe defied the direct order of Prime Minister Naoto Kan *not* to use seawater to cool the reactor. Perhaps the prime minister was thinking of the twelve thousand tons of radioactive water that would spill back into the sea: Most people seem to have forgotten about the cesium, strontium, and plutonium in all those thousands of tons of glowing water, more than fifteen thousand terabecquerels of radiation now swilling around the world's oceans.

Just as few think anymore about the tens of thousands of terabecquerels of radiation released into the Earth's atmosphere when we vented the reactors.

☞ ☜

But I know this, Himamari: *Not one person*—except me—thinks about the day your father walked into a hospital lobby in Kyoto two months later.

Kazuhiko Kokubo, the engineer who volunteered to enter the reactor and turn the vent wheel with your father, was dying of radiation poisoning, and your father went there to honor him and say good-bye. The official line was that Kazuhiko had a preexisting illness. When your father arrived, he was told in the lobby that Kazuhiko had died an hour earlier, and that he could not see the body, as it was classified as radioactive waste. On the way back to his car your father collapsed, and from his hospital bed he called me on his cell phone. The call wasn't a surprise. For two months your father had done nothing but work to stabilize Fukushima Daiichi. I worked alongside him, and saw his hair fall out onto the desk in his office. But he just swiped the hanks into a trash can and refused to see a doctor. The only thing on his desk now—and it was always piled high with reports in the past—was the childhood picture of you with the tomatoes. When I arrived at the hospital the doctors told me he had days to live, perhaps just hours.

I found your father naked on his hospital bed, his legs and arms spread wide. His skin—covered in pimpled red sores—was open and oozing. There was gray skin falling in sheets off the foot that had taken the *beta* burn.

He—through blistered lips—asked me to find *you*.

I sprinted to the parking lot.

In Tokyo, everyone was wearing masks. At Babylon 666, the owner told me you had quit your band and were working at a "Citizens Radiation Monitoring Station" and gave me directions to a local supermarket, where I found you running a primitive Geiger counter over the groceries of a long line of frightened mothers, many with masked children in hand. Two of the children had nosebleeds while I stood there waiting for you to finish your shift. I helped one mother with her bleeding child. She was so upset she could not even think to sit the child down and have her tip her head back. But then the child's nose didn't stop bleeding, and I said something to the frantic mother like, "This works normally."

And then you looked over and said, "Normal is no longer normal."

The child's mother was breaking down as the nosebleed worsened, and the hysteria was spreading to those women in line to have their groceries checked for radiation. I suggested we take the child to a hospital, and the four of us got into your father's car.

And it was then I told you about your father.

It was then you told me about your abortion.

The gold was gone from your hair, and you were wearing jeans, a T-shirt, and a cotton *hachimaki* that held your hair back neatly from your face.

You spoke nonstop all the way to Kyoto Hospital of the cesium in breast milk, of thyroid exposure, of wildly fluctuating levels of radionuclides on fruits, vegetables, and rice, of how mothers-to-be counted the fingers and toes on the ultrasounds of their babies-to-be, of the uncertainty and invisible threat of strontium and plutonium breaking DNA strands, and how the slow, creeping psychological pressure and lack of control were pushing people you knew into listlessness, depression, and addiction, about how every conversation was about *Where were you on March 15 when the radiation reached Tokyo, and what did your children eat and drink that day?*

You spoke of government lies and cover-ups, and how the Japanese couldn't think for themselves, and how you didn't know what to do, and how that was killing you. At the time it didn't cross my mind that when you *did* decide what to do, it *would* kill you.

As I sped north to Osaka—hoping we made it in time for you to say good-bye to your father—I remember you kept repeating under your breath: *The ordinary is over.*

Just as I turned into the hospital, almost hitting an ambulance, you turned to me and said, "I don't even know your name."

I was about to tell you, but you suddenly held your hands over your ears and said not to speak.

You then looked at me and said, "I will call you 'Eri.'"

I liked that name: *My Protector.*

That was the first of two names you would dub me with over the next months. I wish you had never given me the second.

Your father was not dead, but when we entered his room he was fully dressed, sitting in a yellow chair, waiting for you, Himamari.

He bowed to you and asked to be taken home to his farm. His desire to check out of the hospital caused a small uproar, and in the end I had to ram your father in his wheelchair past a crowd of doctors, nurses, and hospital executives. He laughed about it as we drove north, and asked over and over in a whispery voice if I was in the Mafia. It was his Italian thing. But I had signed in the visitor's ledger when I went to the hospital and put down that I worked for TEPCO at Fukushima Daiichi, and there would be swift fallout—so to speak—from my actions in freeing your father.

An hour later we came to the police blockade at the edge of the twelve-mile radiation evacuation zone around Fukushima Daiichi. I rolled down your father's window, and he flashed his work badge at the policemen, and they saluted him as a high executive, said "*Hai!*" and raised the barrier. We passed towns that were nothing but wood and rubble, and we stopped for cows lying in the street. The cows had been freed before the farmers fled, and now many were fat on the grass and enjoying the warmth of the asphalt. What we didn't know was how many hundreds had died of starvation, chained in their stalls. We also saw dozens of orphaned dogs and cats roaming the ruins.

Soon after that an ostrich blocked our way. The ostrich was the symbol of TEPCO, and this one, kept around for corporate events, had somehow gotten free.

Your father said quietly, "The ostrich is like TEPCO: It sticks its head in the sand when there is danger." He looked at me and laughed quietly, and I saw that even laughing was causing him a great deal of pain.

At the farm, you and I helped your father from the car. For a moment he stood erect, but then he slumped against you and slid to the ground. You got the wheelbarrow from the garden and filled it with pillows. I placed your father in the wheelbarrow and, taking the two handles, rolled him up his driveway. Your father raised his hand as we turned toward the farmhouse, and you bent down to his lips and then said, "He wants to go to the garden."

You took a handle of the wheelbarrow, and together we rolled your father to the garden. When we came to the wooden gate, he raised his hand and pointed, so we pushed the wheelbarrow over the soft soil, between the rows of tomato plants. The garden—despite the earthquake and tsunami and nuclear meltdown—was neatly planted and growing. Your father must have tended it when he got home from work each night, but he must have done it at times by the light of his truck headlights. I saw you look around, then bend over and cup a tiny green tomato in your hand.

Your father motioned to get out of the wheelbarrow, and you ran to the farmhouse and returned with blankets and more pillows, and we made a bed in the garden, and together placed him gently on it. It was late that night, surrounded in the dark by green tomatoes, with you holding his hand, that he died. I lay on the hood of the car that night, close enough to hear you singing to your father. I remember you singing Judy Mowatt's "I Shall Sing" over and over, and you told me later your father pressed your hand as a sign to sing it again.

In the morning, I walked over to the garden and found you asleep with your head on your father's chest. I stood and looked at the golden sunflower medallion around your neck as it glittered in the sunrise.

You awoke when a dog missing a leg—with the bone showing—ran barking past the garden, and you went in the farmhouse and brought out tea. You said someone needed to care of all the animals left behind, as they were "sentient beings." I knew the water in your well was probably very radioactive. We sipped the tea, and you told me about the Rastafarian idea of "sitting in the dirt": a way of awakening to nature and getting away from the corrosive "doing"-oriented mind-set of all that is *Babylon.*

Then you told me about the Japanese idea of *teikkai,* of knowing where your food was grown, how it was grown, and who grew it. You plucked a green tomato and bit into it. I wanted to stop you, or tell you to wash it with bottled water from the car, as I could almost see the radioactive isotopes.

I suspected then how this would end. That in less than a year I would return here, and alone dig a second grave in the garden.

There were blue flies landing on your father, and I told you about Kazuhiko Kokubo, and how his body was classified as radioactive waste and taken away. You stood, walked to an outbuilding, and came back with two shovels. Together we dug a grave in the path between the tomatoes. As I dug I thought about how we were at the very heart of the twelve-mile radiation exclusion zone, and how the Japanese government said no one would be able to live here again for thirty years. I had glanced at my dosimeter back at the car, and your farm was at forty-five millisieverts, one of the hottest spots in the hot zone. Raising my eyes as I dug, I could see what you avoided looking at as a little girl: the gray boxes of the nuclear reactors at Fukushima Daiichi.

We placed your father at the bottom of the grave in a sheet, and you turned away as I covered him with dirt. When the dirt was level, you replanted six small tomato plants in a neat row down the length of his body.

You got a guitar from the house, and sang over the grave. It was your song "Durty Gul," and I remember the lines:

> I walk on air
> From mountaintop to mountaintop
> Dirt in my hands
> I walk on air with flowers in my hair

BAGRAM

The four soldiers from the 519th Military Intelligence Unit got a room at the Holiday Inn. At 3:00 a.m. he came back to the hotel room alone and sat in the dark. He went to the door and got down like a dog and sniffed and then shoved wet towels under in case the smell was coming from the hallway. Later through the wall he heard a child and he broke some soap off a bar and warmed it in his palms, rolled a couple of white marbles, and plugged his ears. He could still hear the child, and when a second child started up—it sounded like a girl—it was too much and he took a knife and cut his shoulder where there was a lot of scar tissue. He ended up drinking tequila—because he had once heard it was more drug than booze—in a park near the Potomac and at dawn stripped down and tried to swim across the river.

Commuters spotted him from the bridge and the cops fished him out. He said, "I'm just back from Afghanistan" and laughed. Shivering he stood at parade rest on the deck of the boat and he was bigger than any of the cops, and they were big men. One cop tossed him a gray blanket. When the boat landed he shrugged off the blanket, jumped onto the dock, and two cops grabbed him, and then it took four to get him in cuffs. The cops apologized and took him to Walter Reed, the military hospital. He was treated for hypothermia and when he didn't speak they put him in a locked psychiatric ward. It was a *protest*, not speaking, although he couldn't say against *what* exactly. He liked that the metal doors were locked and there were guards. There was a crack under the door. He didn't like that air could slip under that crack. The nurses saw him at times walking around sniffing the room with a look of terror. Black hair cut in a slab, blue eyes smiling, the body of a once-champion Georgetown University shot-put thrower infantilized by a hospital johnny, but except for those moments of sniffing and the not talking, he *looked* OK. He looked impish and boyish and openly friendly, weird in such a large man. Only he *had* jumped into the Potomac, and the only time he spoke was to tell a nurse—after he was accidentally given an antipsychotic meant for a marine convinced he had cloven feet—that he had gone in because "she was afraid of drowning."

The nurse said he was free to go, that there was no legal reason to keep him, once he answered two questions: *Did he have any desire to harm himself? Did he have any desire to harm anyone else?* Joey shook his head. The thing he was sure of after Bagram: nobody would hurt anyone on his watch ever again, especially a woman or child. This time, he would die before he let that happen. That vow kept him from drinking pesticide one night in Bagram. "Well, then, Sergeant Withers, you are free to go. Jersey is waiting to take you home." He wondered how they figured out his name, then remembered they took his photo. Computers know all. He could never escape them. As for Jersey, he had never met her. All he knew was that while he was in Afghanistan his personal-trainer brother Andy had married a super-rich twenty-eight-year-old named Arizona with two kids by who knows who, and that Jersey was her smoking-hot little sister.

Jersey looked sixteen at best, and was falling out of a yellow tank top that said QUESTION PATERNITY!, jeans she barely fit in, and wobbling on heels as long as his middle finger. She was a soldier in Afghanistan's wet dream, he was stone, and he knew now—it was becoming clear with each ticking minute back in America—that he was *not not not* OK. "We're going to Kennebunkport," she said as she led him to a yellow Hummer, and when Joey just smiled, she added, "Didn't Andy tell you *anything* about us Masuccis? That's where your brother and Arizona live now since my parents died, in our old summer house, right across the little bay from the Bush compound. You can watch them through a telescope on the porch. My parents used to go to dinner over there once or twice a summer because my father owned a company that did things for the government. OK, truth alert: he was CIA." When Joey just tilted his head at this news, she added, "And just so you know, it's pretty much going to be just you and me and the two kids most of the time. The old house, it can be creepy, so I'm glad you're here to be the guy. You'll keep us safe with those biceps, right? Arizona isn't much for the mother thing and pretty much stays in St. Barts or the Seychelles or someplace far away with Andy, but I absolutely love getting to be their mother because they are just like innocent fucking angels, two of the most beautiful children in the world." Then she turned and smiled and said, "And you look like you can play the role of Daddy. Your brother never showed any interest, but they aren't *his* kids, and she married him to be her bodyguard, not their father, to pull her out of shit when they have too much fun in the sun. Arizona never told me you were so hot. How fucking big are your arms? Can I ask how many terrorists you killed? Arizona said you were some kind of American hero. I wish my daddy could have met you: he was all about soldiers and killing terrorists and all that violent shit."

Jersey talked all the way up 95. Joey was sure the chatter was an act. Her eyes were saying more than her mouth, and if he had to choose one word he'd say she was *scared*. He vowed in his head to protect her and these two unnamed kids, and sighed loudly, grateful that someone was giving him a second chance. Jersey glanced at his chest and said nothing. He opened and shut the window a few times, closing his eyes to the rush of warm air.

As the Hummer entered New York, Joey asked his first question: Jersey replied that although her sister was *her* legal guardian since their parents' deaths in the crash of her father's small plane on their horse farm in Virginia, *she* had unofficially been mother to Arizona's kids Annapolis and Kenny for the last six months. Joey nodded and gazed out the window at the skyline of Manhattan and clenched his nails into his palms. Unlike most of the 519th Military Intelligence Unit at Bagram, he hadn't signed up because the Twin Towers went down. He had signed up because Mrs. Hachi, his ninth-grade Global Studies teacher at Bethesda High, had made him do a report on women in Afghanistan under the Taliban, and the stuff he read had flipped him out. At Georgetown he studied International Relations and was the only man in a college chapter of the Revolutionary Association of the Women of Afghanistan. He secretly dated an Afghani-American woman named Alissa until her brothers found out and she was forced to drop out of college. He tracked her down and stood outside her double-decker house in a rough section of Philadelphia until her five brothers came out with knives and told him if he persisted they would kill her. Then the towers went down, then Bush went into Afghanistan, then he dropped out and joined the army to help the women of Afghanistan. The Army put him in an intelligence unit when it was clear how much he knew about Afghanistan. Most soldiers couldn't locate the country on a map: He knew the names and personal histories of the top Taliban leaders and knew from Alissa conversational Dari and even a little Pashto. He looked down at his hands. His palms had stopped bleeding and now were callused over, so recently he had been chewing on his tongue until it bled in his mouth, and now he had a huge electric canker right on the tip, too. He sniffed Afghanistan in the air—although it might have been the black diesel cloud ahead—and ran the window up, turned on the air-conditioning. He glanced out the back of the Hummer a few dozen times until Jersey said, "Whoa, Joey honey, the war is over for you."

At a rest stop in Massachusetts she bought some Twizzlers. When she returned he was standing by the hood looking at two children walking with their mother, and right then the mother flipped him off. Joey put his unshaven face in his hands, and Jersey rubbed his arm, the one with the 519th tattoo. Jersey said, "People do that all the time. They think we're rich assholes for driving a Hummer. But we Masuccis *are* rich assholes. You can't pick your parents, right? I mean, fuck them, Daddy had to do a lot of bad shit to make his money." She drove her head down in his lap and blew on him through his camos and said, "You need a little road head from your hot underaged girlfriend to help you chill." She unzipped him and pulled his cock upright like she was dangling a snake by the head and kissed his shaft, but after a while she stopped, and when she let go he fell over. "Timber," she said as she made him flop over a few more times. He opened the door of the Hummer and puked and retched for a few minutes as Jersey slipped her surprisingly cold hands up the back of his t-shirt and rubbed his back.

Joey drove the Hummer from the rest stop north to Maine. It felt good to be behind the wheel of a civilian vehicle, even a Hummer. At a BP in Kennebunk, Jersey handed him a credit card to get gas, but it was rejected. She said, "Arizona sometimes forgets to pay. She gets money each month from the trust fund. She's kind of sloppy about paying my credit card, or even putting money in my account."

Joey pulled out his pockets and said, "Before I left Afghanistan I gave all my pay from two years to an orphanage in Kabul. And the cash in my wallet went away when I jumped in the Potomac."

"Shit. You're totally broke?"

"Yes," said Joey. "I brought nothing back but my skin and bones."

Jersey looked at him for a moment, then leaned over and checked the gas gauge. "Well, we're pretty close to my house, but the way this yellow monster chews gas, might be close. But my house has extra fridges and freezers in the basement full of food, steaks, beers, and wine, so we're cool for a month or more, or until Arizona gets sober and does her banking. Daddy was always prepared for the worst. He said if it got really bad, he'd take us over to hide out with the Bushes."

"What was he expecting to happen?"

"Daddy said, 'Someday the chickens are going to come to roost.'"

"And that means?"

"Fuck if I know," said Jersey.

The house in Kennebunkport sprawled for a hundred salty, shingled yards on the Maine shoreline. Jersey said it was worth eight million. Joey parked the Hummer outside the ten-car garage. Tour buses were parked below them at a pullover on Scenic 1A. Jersey pointed at a bulb of land in the Atlantic covered with nondescript houses. "That's the Bush compound. People from all over the country stop night and day to look over like they might see Jesus playing tennis with old King George.

I grew up hanging out with their grandchildren over there in the summers, and that's what his grandchildren called him: King George. You'd
think as the leaders of the free world they'd be classy, but they were
crude and hostile, you know? But my father always made me go over
there to play in a nice dress for business reasons. Arizona one summer
had sex a lot with a couple of the Bush cousins, which I think Daddy
approved of, but I thought they were all pigs."

Joey got out of the Hummer and ran. He leapt onto a perfect rock
wall and vaulted over the spikes of the metal gate. Jersey yelled to him.
He crossed Scenic 1A as a tour bus pulled up. He walked down a dirt
path to stand on a giant slab of granite that jutted over the Atlantic.
Dark rollers broke on the shore below, sending salt spray into his face.
He picked up a chunk of rock the size of a softball, weighed it in his
hand, then wound up, spun around, and sent it arcing over the water
toward the Bush compound. The compound was hundreds of yards
away, and his rock fell harmlessly into the sea, but it felt good—such
a release of what was devouring him—so he did it again, then again.
Just as he was coiling up again he felt a soft hand on his bicep. Tourists stared at him and stepped back as Jersey led him across the street,
through the oxide-colored iron gate that opened when Jersey punched
in the code and then noiselessly clicked shut behind them, and the two
walked back up the driveway. Jersey held his hand. He turned once
to look back at the Bush compound, then caught the smell of burning
flesh and leaned over and vomited again. There was an ice pick of pain
in his skull. It was real, overwhelming, and out of his control. He fell to
his knees and rolled his forehead on the cobblestones and then banged
his skull hard, and only stopped when he realized there was something
soft between his skull and stone, and opening his eyes he saw Jersey's
bloodied hand.

At Kennebunk Hospital the X-rays showed Jersey had broken the
middle finger of her left hand. Doctor Melmor with a social worker
named Diane quizzed Jersey on domestic abuse. They had seen Joey's
forehead—which looked like it was spread with strawberry jam—in the
waiting room. He had refused treatment and sat holding paper towels

to his head and asking the nurses every five minutes how Jersey was doing and when she would be out.

Jersey told them to just please finish setting her finger. When she came out to the waiting room she had her hand behind her back, then pulled it out to display her raised middle finger to Joey. It was taped to a silver splint and wrapped in white tape.

"Fuck you, Joey," she said laughing. "Nice way to start our life together."

Joey ran over and took her hand in his and said, "I'm sorry, Jersey. You have no idea. Does it hurt?"

"I made them give me codeine," said Jersey. "I took a couple, and am due for a third, in my medical opinion. I'm feeling pretty fucking fine, actually." She wrapped her arms around Joey and said, "From here on in, no more banging your skull on the driveway, OK? Just be the man of the family and keep me and the kids safe, OK? The world sucks."

"I promise," said Joey. "I really want to make it all better."

After Joey parked the Hummer again in front of the garage, Jersey walked with him to the front door. There she popped in the code, pushed opened the door, but stopped and said, "I love codeine. Carry me over the threshold like I'm a bride."

Joey laughed and said, "You're crazy, Jersey."

"It's going to be like a movie," said Jersey as Joey scooped her up in his arms. "My big, handsome soldier husband is just back from Afghanistan, but with a little PTSD. I'm a rich girl with a big heart, and will love it out of him, and we will live happily ever after having hot sex and watching Netflix after the kids are safely tucked in for the night. Do you want to be cast in this movie, Joey?"

"You have no idea how much," said Joey, and he stepped, with her in his arms, into the huge dark foyer. Ahead, with the lights from Route 1A, he saw a giant white marble staircase. It shimmered, like something out of a dream.

"Spin me around, Joey!" cried Jersey, so Joey spun her around and thought to himself: *I can be OK! I can be OK!* Then he spun to the floor, and the two lay in an X beneath the chandelier until Joey stood up and tried to flip the light switches he found by brushing the wall with his fingers. There were eight switches, none worked.

Jersey listened to the switches flipping and said from the floor, "The power has probably been cut off again."

"Arizona didn't pay?" said Joey.

"Portland Electric sucks it from the account automatically when there is money in there," said Jersey. "But you're getting the picture. It's summer, so we won't freeze. And the fridges and stove all run on gas, and the tank is huge and full. And we have candles and flashlights and even hurricane lamps."

"So we live in the dark in this eight-million-dollar house?" said Joey.

"Just at night," said Jersey. "The sun comes up tomorrow, Joey."

"Wait, you said your dad was Mr. End Times," said Joey. "He must have had a diesel generator for this place. It's probably in the garage."

"There is a huge generator," said Jersey. "And a huge underground tank behind the garage for it. But the tank cracked over the winter, and now it's empty."

Two little shadows ran in and jumped on top of Jersey on the hall floor. A flashlight played over the three of them, and Jersey's silver finger splint flashed in the light. A woman in the doorway said in a Jamaican accent, "They miss you, Miss Jersey. I'll come over and talk tomorrow, but I have to rush right back and get the Malloys' dinner on the table."

Jersey ran over and hugged the maid and said, "Thank you so much, Harvette. Is it OK if I pay you when Arizona gives me some money again?"

Harvette gave Jersey a hug and said, "Don't you worry about that. You know I love those children." She turned to go and then—after insisting on handing over her flashlight—said, "Oh, only other news is there was a big storm off the ocean this morning, and you lost that apple tree in the backyard to lightning, the one you used to play on when you were a little girl."

The kids begged to see the "lightning tree," and Annapolis jumped up and down when Joey said he was game. She jumped in his arms, and he swung her up to sit on his shoulder. Kenny took the flashlight and led them out and around the house, through two picket gates, and under an arch covered in vines.

The lightning had destroyed the tree, and the scorched trunk was still warm. A large limb was on the ground, and trapped under it an old wooden swing-set seat. Kenny yanked at the seat, and when Joey helped him, the board snapped in two. Annapolis burst into tears and lay on the lawn and blamed Joey in a rising storm of outrage first for breaking the swing-set seat, then for the destroyed apple tree (her favorite for climbing), then for Jersey going away and her mother never calling and traveling all the time. She flailed back and forth, pulled her hair and screamed that she wanted to *die right now* and *someone should throw her off the roof of the house.*

Jersey asked Joey to pick her up from the lawn, and when he lifted the little girl she screeched *"No, no, no don't touch me!"* like he was burning her. He put Annapolis in Jersey's outstretched arms—careful of her broken finger—and she carried her up to the house. Kenny walked before them with the flashlight, holding it upright like a torch.

Joey sat on a broken limb of the apple tree and watched the flashlight move through the empty house. Soon they were in a room on the second floor. He raised his hands and looked at them in the moonlight: They were shaking. The screeching of Annapolis was still in his head, as was the screeching of another little girl, and the different screams of a little boy: Those screams he had heard for months, had listened to them and the wailing and curses in Dari from their mother while slumped against the wall outside their cell in the prison at Bagram.

He reached along the ground and picked up the broken swing-set seat, stuck out his leg and brought the board down hard against his muscular thigh. He raised it higher and hit harder, the way they did to the mother as she hung naked from the ceiling, until her thighs were pulpified. Blood poured into his mouth as he bit down on his tongue, and then he suddenly smelled something burning, and he looked up.

Then he dropped the board.

She had followed him here.

There was a hexagonal glass cupola set on the roof of the house. The moonlight was stronger now, or maybe it was the light from 1A. But the mother, Hama, was up there in the cupola, looking down at him in the backyard.

☞ ☜

The sun came up the next morning, as Jersey had promised. It was bright and hard and glared in because there were no curtains.

The enormous master bedroom looked out over the Atlantic, and also at the Bush compound. Joey stared. A man was over there painting lines on a green tennis court. It looked like he was putting up a net. Joey closed his eyes and winced. His thigh was twitching, and there was a sodden ache from his knee to his crotch. He remembered feeling his way up the staircase in the dark and slipping into bed next to Jersey, and how she cried out during the night when he rolled over on her broken finger, and the sound of her sleeping cry gave him a flashover of pain. She must have felt him trembling as he lay on his back in the dark, so she hugged him until she fell asleep again. Her holding him made it much worse. Her breasts on his chest were an accusation.

Joey hadn't closed his eyes. He was on Code Red alert all night, drilling a hole into the darkness of a mansion in Maine. Hama was like a match to a body filled with kerosene. He tried deep breathing. He tried happy memories. He kept thinking about the cupola and Hama. He kept thinking about the can of pesticide he kept in his room at Bagram. He raised his hands: They were shaking. He looked around the room, and that was when he awoke to the fact it was a construction zone. Not only were there no curtains, but the floors were plywood, the walls stripped of wallpaper (a few strips remained, sort of pink and green floral thing), and one whole wall was naked two-by-fours, so you could see into what he guessed was another bedroom, and from that bedroom and from between the two-by-fours emerged Annapolis.

In the dark the night before he had not been able to see her, but now before him stood a thin little girl of five or so with tangled brown hair down to her waist. She had matted locks like a Rastafarian. She studied him with unnerving blue cat eyes. She walked over in an adult T-shirt with red block letters that said KENNEBUNK RESCUE and then somersaulted onto the bed. She stood up and started to bounce, and Jersey groaned and said *Let me sleep let me sleep.* She opened one eye and said to Joey, "Would you be my darling husband and take her downstairs for some breakfast?" Joey felt a balm pass into him: Maybe this day could be calm and normal. Like he was a dad and husband and was on call to make his little girl breakfast like he did every day.

Joey, still fully dressed, slid his legs over the side of the bed. He knew it was going to hurt when he put pressure on his leg, but the pain in his thigh collapsed the knee, and he slid to the floor. Annapolis bounced off the bed and climbed onto his back. She said *You're a giant monster and I'm a fairy princess!* Jersey had sat up to see if he was OK, and Joey just said his leg was asleep, then rose with Annapolis clinging to his back. He hitched the little girl up onto his shoulders, the smile from Jersey quieted his racing heart, and he vowed to see that smile a hundred times this day.

"Annapolis and I will be downstairs making breakfast," said Joey. "Your job is to go back to bed. Send Kenny down if he wakes up."

"Kenny sleeps like a dead man," said Annapolis.

Joey looked at Jersey. It seemed a weird thing for a kid to say. "Her grandfather used to say that about Kenny," said Jersey.

Joey nodded and let out a giant's roar, and Annapolis cried out in mock fear, and the two headed out of the bedroom. Jersey called after them, "I'm going to marry you Joey, you know!"

The hallway looked like someone had marched down it swinging a wrecking ball. Sheetrock was ripped down in some places; in other places there were just two-by-fours, or no wall at all. Yellow insulation was hanging out all over. Some walls were splashed with color samples (mostly Easter-egg shades), others had been used as easels by Annapolis and Kenny.

"What's going on?" said Joey.

"My mummy is redecorating," said Annapolis.

"I'll say," said Joey.

On the landing, Joey looked through a stained-glass window at the remains of the apple tree in the backyard. He looked for another tree to put up a swing set for the children. There were no obvious candidates; all the other trees were slender birch plantings, still staked with wires.

He saw a dozen grassless landing zones covered in sawdust: Someone had chain-sawed some big trees and clawed up their root balls.

"Mummy said the house was too dark," said Annapolis.

The downstairs was cannibalized. It was all fresh two-by-four walls and yellow Romex wires and white PVC piping from one end to the other. The house echoed with their footsteps.

"Your mummy really didn't like the house the way it was," said Joey.

"She said it was scary," said Annapolis.

The kitchen was mostly just a boxed two-by-four zone with an industrial-sized stainless silver fridge, and a new stove. But there were also some ancient beams pegged together post-and-beam style. He reached up and touched some marks on the darkened, beaten wood.

"Those were made by slaves," said Annapolis.

Joey drew back his hand. "How do you know?"

"Grandpa said all the old wood came from a ship that had slaves."

And then there was the mess. Joey shook his head: There was garbage all over the floor, flowing out of black plastic bags. Food wrappers and containers, Chinese takeout containers by the dozens, all mixed in with cardboard boxes overflowing with clothes and toys, movies and DVDs. The chaos rattled him, and he didn't want to be more rattled today. He was the sort of man who cleaned up his perimeter as he cooked: and he had always liked to cook. He was the one in his family who got up early and prepared the whole Thanksgiving meal. As a boy he had started making garlic mashed potatoes, and it just evolved into his thing. He had stopped cooking, of course, in Afghanistan, and in the end almost stopped eating; he dropped thirty pounds in the final month. The smell of burning meat made him sick, and since he had come back to America, he seemed to smell it in the air. Annapolis was kicking her heels into him like he was a pony. There were a few flies circling him. He swatted at them and stopped breathing.

The garbage bags were moving.

"The rats got into the garbage again," said Annapolis.

"Rats?"

"Shake a garbage bag."

Joey kicked a bag, and for a second nothing happened. Then two black rats shot out, fired across the floor, and disappeared down a large hole in the floor open to the basement where there must have been stairs, but now there was just a paint-stained wooden ladder poking up.

Annapolis cried out, "Run, ratties, run!"

As Joey kicked other bags, more rats poked out their whiskered heads, then threw themselves headlong into the dark of the basement. Annapolis was shrieking in delight.

"Jesus," said Joey. "I hate rats. Don't they scare you?"

Annapolis was quiet and then said, "They used to. But now you're here."

Joey's knees almost buckled, and he took a deep breath. It was all very weird with the rats and garbage, and well, everything, but now he had a job to do. Somehow, it was an antidote. "First, we police this kitchen area and get rid of the garbage ASAP," said Joey. "That will help with the rats. Then, breakfast. How about pancakes?"

He had spotted some Aunt Jemima mix.

"Yes!" cried Annapolis. "Can I help make them?"

"Can you mix and flip?"

"Yes," said Annapolis. "If you show me."

"Haven't you ever watched Jersey or your mummy cook?"

"We always go out, or get pizza."

Joey tried to slide Annapolis off his back, but she clung tighter. So Joey took out all the garbage bags with a little girl on his back, then cleaned up the garbage from the kitchen floor, put it in empty boxes he found, and hauled them outside.

It was still a bright blue-sky day, with a wind off the Atlantic so strong he almost had to lean into it. He opened his mouth wide and took deep, obvious gulps of the salty air, then went in search of garbage cans. In the garage he found eight silver cans lined up and strapped to the wall with bungee cords, alongside an antique Aston Martin, which was next to a Land Rover, a Jeep, a Ford truck with dual back wheels, a Jaguar, and a Maserati. All the vehicles were lipstick red.

Annapolis rubbed his crew cut the whole time he was transferring the mess into the silver cans. She seemed to be in a trance over the feel of bristle on palm. Joey stacked the boxes filled with garbage from the kitchen floor on top, and when he was done a strange giddiness came over him. He circled all the cars in the garage, then opened the door of the Maserati, plucked Annapolis off his shoulders, and the two climbed in the car. He plopped her in his lap, and he taught her to drive. They drove to Florida, Montana, Iowa: a scenic tour of America. She laughed when he yelled out every thirty seconds or so, spinning his hands over the wheel, "Annapolis, we're going to crash and burn!"

The only way to get her out of the car was to promise to teach her to make the best pancakes in the entire universe. But when he stepped from the Maserati, he noticed a tool shed off the back of the garage, and with Annapolis back on his shoulders, he headed in. The room was full of new carpentry and gardening tools, many still in their boxes or wrappers; there were two sit-down mowers, a chain saw, and a shelves full of paints, shellacs, pesticides, fertilizers, and car fluids. For a few moments he stared at the pesticide, then he grabbed it, walked over to the garbage boxes, and tossed it in, covering it with old magazines. Back in the tool room he grabbed up a box of rat poison and some old-fashioned fly strips, as well as a new garden hose and a sprinkler. He thought Annapolis and Kenny might like it if he set up a sprinkler to run through in the backyard.

Outside, he looked out at a surf rescue boat rowing along the shore. There were two men in it stroking perfectly together, but fighting the wind and waves. When they got near the Bush compound a long gray Zodiac motored slowly out to them, circled, and they changed direction, skirting farther out to sea. Joey looked until Annapolis drove her heels into his chest, and he turned and went in the kitchen. It looked so much better already. He put down Annapolis and the things in his arms and told her to help him find a frying pan, a mixing bowl, some plates, and silverware. While she looked, he grabbed an old bowl off the fridge that was full of postcards, and near the hole in the floor to the basement he poured some rat poison in the bowl, then told Annapolis it was there and to never, ever touch it. Then he placed a couple of fly strips out of sight behind some two-by-fours.

It was hard to find a frying pan. Annapolis and Joey tore through the boxes, but kitchen things were mixed in with toiletries, and these were in turn mixed with old clothes and magazines. It was as if the whole house had been poured randomly into boxes, then all the boxes shaken. But at last they found a cast-iron skillet, a big fruit bowl, and some paper plates. Joey found matches and lit the gas grill, taking time to explain the danger of the pretty blue flame to Annapolis.

The butter sizzled in the skillet, and Annapolis cut off chunks and popped them in her mouth. "Butter hound," said Joey. He let her mix the pancake mix, then showed her how to pour it out carefully so it made little people and animals. Annapolis poured too much on, laughed and added a head, then said, "That's you, Joey." She climbed back on his shoulders when the pancakes were on two plates, and then they carried them up to Jersey, who was sitting up in bed with her arm around a newly awoken Kenny.

"Pancakes!" yelled Annapolis. "And I know how to make them!" She proceeded to tell Kenny all about the process (from the blue gas flame to proper stirring to ladling shapes to flipping when there were bubbles to licking the mixing bowl) with such enthusiasm you would think no one had ever made pancakes before. Jersey was looking at him as if she was going to cry, and then she pulled him by the hand into the bed. The four of them shared the pancakes, with Jersey placing a bite in the mouth of each of them in turn, saying as she presented the fork to the children, "Open up, little birdy."

Jersey looked at him when the pancakes were gone and whispered *You have no idea how special a man you are, Joey.* He closed his eyes, shook his head slowly, got out of the bed, and went out of the bedroom. Jersey called to him, and when he didn't answer, she jumped up and ran after him. She heard the front door open and slam. She ran down the stairs, flung open the door, and called, "Joey!" But he was nowhere, there was just the thrashing sound of a few birds nesting in a lilac bush, the roar of the Atlantic breaking on the rocks across the street. Jersey ran down the cobblestones, slipped quickly through the electric gate as it opened, and ran across Route 1A. Two buses had pulled up and emptied dozens of tourists, and Jersey ran among them, looking for Joey, then ran down to where he had hurled rocks at the Bush compound, and found herself scanning the shoreline, sure for some reason he had flung himself into the Atlantic.

She walked back up to the milling tourists, asked a bus driver if he had seen a big man with a soldier's haircut as they pulled up. He looked up and down the road and at all the elderly tourists, shook his head. Jersey ran back across 1A and climbed over the fence, and that was when she heard the chain saw in the back yard. She found him back there, shirt off, cutting into the apple tree. When she tried to get him to stop he shook his head, but smiled, and then went back to chopping up the tree. She stood staring at him, his extraordinary triceps and deltoids rippling. He only stopped to refill the saw with gas and oil, and when he had reduced the tree to two-foot lengths, he stacked them neatly behind a stone wall.

When he was done stacking, he dragged away the branches, and when the branches were gone, he raked up the leaves, and when the leaves were gone and there was nothing but scraped earth he found grass seed, and with his open palm he sprinkled the seed around, and then the children came over. The three of them tossed grass seed first at the ground, and then, laughing wildly, at each other. It ended when Joey picked up the remains of the blue bag of Agway seed and poured it over the heads of Annapolis and Kenny, and then the two of them chased him around the yard until he let them drag him to the ground.

"I surrender!" Joey yelled, laughing, as Annapolis sat on one of his arms and Kenny sat on his ankles. Annapolis said they would only let him up if he took them for a bike ride, and twenty minutes later, helmets on and with brand-new blue and pink bikes taken down from the hooks in the garage, Jersey walked next to Annapolis holding her upright on her bike, while Joey did the same for Kenny, and the four made their way up Route 1A.

Jersey had snacks and drinks she had shoved in a backpack, and they sat on the rocks over the ocean and had a picnic, then collected periwinkles and Kenny and Annapolis tried for an hour to skip flat stones. When they returned to the house it was dusk, and Joey asked what they wanted for dinner, and it was unanimous: pancakes. Kenny wanted to help make them, but Joey said, "My mother always made us read before we went to bed. Don't you have any books in the house?"

Annapolis yelled, "*Little House on the Prairie!*" and ran over to a box.

She came back waving a book. She pressed it into Joey's hands and said, "Will you read it to us?" Joey took her and Kenny by the hand and led them up to the bedroom. At the landing, Annapolis stopped and said looking out the window, "I miss my swing set in the apple tree," and Joey scooped her up with one arm and said, "I bet one might show up tomorrow."

When the children were in the bed reading with Jersey, Joey went back down and worked on a small stack of pancakes. He found and lit a candle by the flame on the stove, and while a batch of pancakes was cooking, he lit another candle and went down the ladder into the basement. Halfway down, he moved the candle in his fist and saw three or four rats run out of sight. He wondered if any of them had eaten the poison, and promised himself in the morning to sprinkle some down here where it would do the most good. He briefly looked around within the radius of the candlelight at the old stone foundation, at the chisel marks of stonemasons now dead two hundred years or more, found one of the gas-powered fridges and put a beer in each of his back pockets. Then he climbed back up the ladder, flipped the pancakes, and using the same plate from the morning as he couldn't find another, took the stack upstairs.

He could hear Kenny reading from *Little House*. It was a scene in which typhoid breaks out, and Kenny read slowly, with Jersey jumping in when he stumbled over a word. As he entered the room he saw the three of them in the bed, Jersey with her arm around the two readers, and then he dropped the pancakes. He stood yelling loudly at the window, "Oh fuck! Oh fuck!" and then he put his hands on his knees and yelled as if to himself Oh fuck, oh fuck, oh fuck. Annapolis burst into tears and Kenny shouted, "What's wrong?" Joey went out into the hallway, stood there hyperventilating, and when Jersey came out he put his arms around her and said between gasping breaths, "I saw her in the window. She wants the children. She wants Annapolis and Kenny."

Jersey put her hand on Joey's shoulder and said, "Listen to me. Calm down. Take some deep breaths. Nothing followed you back, Joey. You're just freaking out."

Joey pushed past her and went back to the window. He looked out into the darkness and said in a whisper, "I have to keep you safe." Jersey rubbed his back and whispered, "Just keep breathing, Joey. We're all OK. Just keep breathing. The war is over. It's just anxiety. It'll get better." Jersey went back to the children and climbed in next to them and said, "Let's keep reading. Everything is OK."

☞ ☜

Jersey awoke twice. The first time there was only enough light to see Joey sitting up by the window, staring at her with wide eyes. She whispered, "It's all going to be OK," but he just stared back at her. The second time Jersey awoke it was to the sound of sawing. Dawn was breaking over the Atlantic with a yellow-orange haze and clouds that looked like they hadn't moved all night. Jersey slipped sideways from the bed and walked down the stairs, and out the landing window she saw Joey. He was standing in the center of the seeded ground. He had set up two sawhorses, and was hand-sawing through a beam. She stood there and watched as he measured and cut, unable to leave the children alone, as much as she was sure the ghost he had seen the night before was all in his head. He had clearly worked as a carpenter once. It wasn't long before two large A's were lying on the ground, and when he lifted one she knew he was making a new swing set. He placed the crossbar in a notch he had cut at the top of one of the two A's, and when he dropped the other in, she was weeping. He went in the house and came back with the ladder that went to the basement, and climbed up and hammered spikes into the crossbeams. Then he added two support beams to hold up each end, and shook the swing set violently, and then moved the ladder around, adding more and more spikes.

It was the pounding on the spikes that must have awoken Annapolis, and she knew right away what Joey was doing, and jumped up and down and pulled Jersey by the hand. She looked back up at where Kenny was sleeping, but then allowed herself to be pulled outside. The sun was bright, and it was becoming a beautiful summer day in Maine. She went right over to Joey, threw her arms around him, and whispered, "you big lovable bastard." Annapolis came over and wrapped her arms around the two of them, then broke off and said, "Can we put a swing on now?"

Joey nodded and picked up a board from the ground and said, "Isn't this your old swing-set seat?" Annapolis nodded and Joey said, "How about you help me put the ropes in these holes?" The two of them sat on the ground and wove the rope in one hole and pulled it through, then wove it back through another hole and again pulled it through. Then they did the other rope. Joey hoisted Annapolis up, and she dropped the rope over the beam and grabbing the end, pulled it down as Joey lowered her to the ground. He knotted it, and there was the swing. Joey gave it a little push and said Hop on, Annapolis, and she jumped up and yelled I'm first on the swing set!

Joey pushed her higher and higher and told her stories about when he was a boy, how he used to like to leap off at the top of the arc and fly through the air. Annapolis said she wanted to try, and Joey said you have to start with little jumps. He gave her a swing and she jumped off, and then Jersey said she was going to run back in the house and get Kenny. But right then Kenny emerged from the house, carrying a steaming bowl filled with pancakes. Jersey yelled, "You made pancakes? How did you know how to do that?"

Kenny said, "Annapolis told me how to make them, remember? It's easy."

"Did you turn the stove off?" said Joey.

"Of course," said Kenny. Annapolis had already taken the blue bowl from his hands, and was sitting on the ground stuffing her mouth with pancakes, showing everyone her full mouth now and again. She didn't stop until she had eaten almost every last bite, when Joey suddenly ran over and swatted the bowl from her hands and taking her head in one hand, drove two fingers frantically into her mouth.

THE SOUTHERN STRATEGY

I got out of the Tombs for the fifth time in October 2011. The Tombs is a jail in New York City, and the judge, who sat on a little yellow hemorrhoid pillow, must not have had enough fiber the night before and shit broken glass this morning, because she ripped me a new one. She did the old-school penal thing of—in so many words—telling me to get my macrobiotic, unemployed, Occupy Wall Street ass across the state line by sundown or else. It was beautiful in its theatrical way. I held out my wrists the whole time to illuminate Her Highness on the damage from the zipcuffs perpetrated by the police-state thugs. She asked if I had anything to say for myself, so I baffled her with Winston Churchill: "This is not the end. It is not even the beginning of the end. But it is, perhaps, the end of the beginning." Then it was over, and mostly I remember—like it was a silent movie—the comical red O of her lips up there on the legal throne, pursing and popping at me, like a talking asshole.

I said cool about vamoosing by sundown. Like, I was in no mood to hang around NYC anyway, what with Zuccotti Park getting shuttered the night before, with police helicopters overhead and the fascist total embargo put on reporters by the billionaire plutocrat Mayor Bloomberg. I had been peacefully standing on a bench with my iPhone held aloft in my right hand doing a livestream video for the Occupy website while tweeting with my left when I was body-slammed by two beefcake boys in blue who spent a little too much time watching WWF and not enough riffling the Bill of Rights. One dropped a knee into my kidney when I was down, and if I'd had a choice, I think I would have opted to be tased. It hurt. Bad. Despite the pain, I wheezed out some Emma Goldman to the cop on my back: "If I can't dance, it's not my revolution!" He missed the irony—as clearly I couldn't dance right then—and slipped his baton around my neck, temporarily incapacitating my right to free speech.

Outside the courthouse, I put on my black skullcap and waggled my front tooth with my tongue, while savoring the free warmth of the winter sun as I weighed my options. Some fellow Occupiers had been freed just before me, and all were standing on the sidewalk jazzing about the next best move. That was the anarchistic beauty of this movement: There was no leader. It was all about horizontal discussion—that's not pillow talk, by the way (though that was a side benefit)—and finding consensus without a vertical power structure. It was a double shot of 100%–pure democracy that had me manic with Athenian energy. It dropped the scales from my eyes, and I burned in my bones with a killer rage at what the corporate-capitalist-military-industrial oligarchs had stolen from all American citizens. In Zuccotti, I had a revelation that revolutionized my soul, and it felt *good*. The night before the final raid, I took out my various pharmaceuticals and ground those candy-colored pills beneath the iron heel of my black jackboots. As I stood outside the courthouse right then, I symbolically ground my boot into the sidewalk again as a tribute to my new liberation, raised my fist in the air and proclaimed those five-century-old poetic words:

> Stone walls do not a prison make,
> Nor iron bars a cage;
> If I have freedom in my heart,
> And in my soul am free,
> Angels alone, that soar above,
> Enjoy such liberty!

A couple of my fellow Occupiers gave me a high five for oratory, so I declaimed it again louder, and when they looked confused this time,

I yelled, perhaps too testily, "Lovelace, people! 1642! From 'To Althea, from Prison'!"

There is a pretty good reason why, three hours later, I was crossing the George Washington Bridge and escaping Manhattan on a brand-new yellow Trek bicycle. I refuse on principle to use gas—or oil-based—transportation. Other reasons include: the bike was left unlocked on top of a Mercedes with a Romney for President sticker while double-parked on Fifth Avenue; a sudden urge to feel the wind in my face after so many months of standing around in Zuccotti Park; and a soul-torching sense that the Occupy movement had hit a brick wall.

Halfway across the bridge, while dodging two mothers both with twin strollers and almost sailing into traffic, I had a eureka of me biking across the back roads of America on the same beautiful yellow bicycle. I believe in following flashes of inspiration, and this vision of me crossing the amber-waves-of-grain states was so clear and strong and pressing. My visions become more elaborate over time, too. And one has to quiver in the *now* and be open to flux at a moment's notice. Openness to the universal message is key. It was on the bridge that I knew that my calling was less the amber waves of grain, and more cottony, and that I should head to the Deep South, that there was some heavenly reason—other than that the wind in my face was bitter—that my future was to be found somewhere in the former Confederacy. As I left the bridge I was so pleased with my new plans that there was nothing to do but declaim a little of the Puritan poet George Herbert:

> I struck the board and cried, "No more!
> I will abroad!
> What, shall I ever sigh and pine?
> My lines and life are free, free as the road,
> Loose as the wind . . ."

I always liked Herbert because, like me with my psychologically enslaved pre-Zuccotti need for a cocktail of mood adjusters, he suffered his whole life with illness, and yet in three years of work fulfilled a great purpose. Now I was giddy with the crystal truth that my great life purpose lay somewhere south, and I sang out Herbert's inspirational words, and each time I recited the first line, I raised my right hand and on the word *struck* gave the handlebar a rhythmic smack with my open palm, and with rising excitation I smacked and sang until I smacked so hard the wheel viciously twisted in my left hand, and the bike and I sailed sideways over a barrier, and into the George Washington's rush-hour traffic.

☞ ☜

The yellow Trek was a pretzel wedged deep under a tractor trailer, and as I limped away I listened to it scrape along the roadway. The scraping was a sort of industrial-inspirational music: a mere bicycle could grind Manhattan rush hour to a halt. All those poor human cogs of the worldwide ravaging capitalist machine, stopped in their busy locust-like lives of plundering the world's last beauties by thirty ounces of tangled, slender metal. It prompted the question: What could I achieve with my 180 pounds of flesh? As I walked, I calculated my physical body was over 4,500 ounces of activist flesh.

Injured flesh, I was realizing. I limped south along the highway as darkness fell on New Jersey, and it grew clearer that the adrenaline of the accident had masked a certain amount of bodily damage. My knee was freezing up with each step, and soon I was hobbling along like Ahab, swinging my bad leg forward with each step. But this, strangely, I sort of enjoyed, in a kinky way. The song "I Will Survive" by Gloria Gaynor popped into my head, and I hobbled along to that disco beat for a few miles as the gladiators of global warming zooming by flicked on their headlights. I have always had a high threshold for physical pain (my Achilles heel has always been emotional-spiritual pain) and for years found some salvation in extreme sports, such as ultramarathons, and in the past ran a hundred-miler, the Leadville Trail race in Colorado, which I finished in twenty-five hours, running through the night at an average elevation of eight thousand oxygen-depleted feet above sea level, and in the twenty-third hour coming into an awakening concerning the illusion of my flesh, which was pure and holy, and which I held to my heart when my sole sibling Margaret called me a fool, and maybe even insane, when she visited me in the hospital in Denver the next day, where I recovered from a stress-related kidney collapse that required a few weeks of dialysis. We hadn't talked since—that was a few years ago—when she and her husband James, the hard-boiled Baptist minister, covered my twenty-thousand-dollar hospital bill, and I refused to promise not to run ultramarathons again and to get a steady job.

It was dusk now as I marched along the highway with my stiff-legged gait, and I found myself loudly singing the "Battle Hymn of the Republic" to crowd out the whine of winter tires on a treeless roadway. Over and over, I sang that old song with its refrain "John Brown's body lies a-mouldering in the grave," and only later did I think how weird it was that I was singing that song on my journey south. For hours I sang and limp-marched to keep my spirits up, and then I admit I started to slide into a minor-key funk, and that had me thinking about what I might want written on my gravestone. I decided on Shakespeare:

> His life was gentle, and the elements
> So mixed in him that Nature might stand up
> And say to all the world, "This was a man."

I see the economic world might find it comical that I wanted to be an ideal "man," but I'd rather this be my goal in life, than to have the Bard say:

> His life was greedy, and devouring
> So dominated in him, that Nature might stand up
> And say to the world, "The worms won't eat this fucker!"

After settling on my epitaph (and hoping it was a bit premature—I was only twenty-eight), it was about midnight when I saw ahead the blinking emergency lights of a van pulled off the highway. The van had a flat on the back left, and a man with a tire iron was having trouble with the lug nuts. I watched him from a dozen feet away, and what I liked right away were the stickers on his green pop-top VW van, and perhaps the largest especially, which read: THIS VAN RUNS ON BIO-

DIESEL. The grease was stored on the roof in a half-dozen blue plastic jugs strapped on with a spider web of bungee cords. It still added to global warming, but to run a vehicle on old French-fry grease showed the driver had some *awakening.*

He was a short but heavily muscular black man with a 1970s afro that looked in the taillights like a red halo, a lumberjack's beard with some gray, and he wore those shiny penny loafers. The loafers were his problem: His shoe kept skidding off the tire iron as he slammed it down. I stepped out of the darkness and gently nudged him aside, and with one sharp kiss of my jackboot broke the nut free. In five minutes he was ready to hit the road with his spare tire, and I was faced with a major-league dilemma: to break my vow not to have a vehicular carbon footprint and contribute to global warming and the end of nature, or to accept a ride. He was about to drive away when I asked where he was going next in his travels on this endangered earth, and he looked at me with kind blue eyes, held my arm tightly, and recited in an amazing bourbon baritone, "*If you, passing, meet me, and should desire to speak to me, why should you not speak to me?*"

I said, "Whitman, 'To You,' 1860."

"Very good," he said. "You a grad student?"

"No," I said.

"You were an English major in college?"

"No," I said. "I don't even have a GED."

"But you know the god Walt?"

Now this I have always found a little baffling and more than a bit irritating: the idea that to know anything about anything nowadays, you have to be in some official school, and not doing it out of pure unfiltered curiosity, or maybe *love.* He saw the look on my face and said, "I get it, man, you just like to *read.*"

I nodded and said, "Exactly. But I read to learn how to *live.*"

"So did you go to college?"

"Not exactly."

"Why not?"

"Loans," I said. "Fuck the banksters. The library is free."

He nodded and said, "So do you want a ride?"

I looked at his van, and was still wavering on my commitment to the dying planet versus getting to that major epiphany waiting to direct my soul south of the Mason-Dixon Line. He nodded and said, "When my trips are over, I plant a tree for every ten miles I travel. Sort of a poor give-back to the Earth."

With that, for the first time in five years, I entered "Machiavelli's spinning-wheel mechanism of world-murder," as I in my more manic moments call any combustion-engine vehicle. It was a bit hard getting my stiff leg up and in, as it had almost locked. And we headed off into the night, jabbering like orphans separated at birth and now reunited by fate on the side of the New Jersey Turnpike via a flat tire.

It turned out Oliver Neville (he liked to be called Neville) was a professor of African American studies at Cornell, and he was on sabbatical. He was a cousin of the singers from New Orleans of the same name.

"But rather than a sabbatical," said Neville, handing me one of those green Grolsch bottles with the porcelain top, "I call it a pilgrimage. I have a couple of sacred spots at which I will pay homage, and hope some grace follows. And that beer in your hand is not a Grolsch, but home-brewed by me with all-organic hops and malt produced locally by a good and noble friend in Ithaca. I added a single sprig of hemlock during the boiling of the hops, as homage to Socrates and the pursuit of truth."

I immediately felt like I was with family, just as I had for those glorious months in Lower Manhattan, where every day I was sure my electric body was burning bright in times as they were finally fucking *a'changing.* Zuccotti Park was like Oxycontin for political dreamers. Truth is, since leaving New York, I'd sensed out there in the vast darkness of corporate-owned America a crouching hurt like a bad withdrawal wanting to devour me, but I was fighting to stay high. Neville reached over and rested his hand on my shoulder as we drove, and my whole body sparked with that gesture of brotherhood. As I got my bearings, I noticed the van's interior was a desolate wreck, as if Neville had tossed all his books and notepads and clothes into the back in big armfuls, then slept on them the three days he'd been on the road.

The van had a good heater—although it blew out a smell of rotting cabbages—and soon I was warm enough to take off the puffy rapper jacket I had gotten at Zuccotti via donation, and Neville saw the hand-drawn design on my T-shirt. Credit to the professor man, he saw it right away.

"Occupy," he said. "Clever graphic."

"Yes," I said. "One day after the big march on the Brooklyn Bridge, while I was in jail for the third time, in my mind I just took the O and put a C inside it, and another C inside that, and then a U inside that, and popped the pi symbol inside that. But you'd be surprised what a big blank it drew with a lot of people."

"Occupy," said Neville, "was a big blank for a lot of Americans."

"People said it would be better if I had a graphic of an apple pie, rather than the pi symbol."

"But all Americans aren't brain-dead," said Neville. "Many get that the proverbial 'apple pie' has been stolen from right under their noses."

"Exactly," I said. "But it's more than economics, you know? Our whole consumptive way of life is evil, murderous, and unsustainable. Everything is terminal, you know?"

"I foresee a revolution on the horizon," said Neville, glancing at me as if to see if I could handle the rough asphalt of truth, pausing, then racing on as he grimaced at the road. "All it needs is a spark, like the one John Brown lit at Harpers Ferry. That raid lit the fuse that led to the Civil War. And what we must have in this country is a new civil war, for once again the great problem in this country is the South. The southern states, their representatives and their people, are blocking, out of a love of ignorance and a warped vision of Jesus, all progress. None of the goals of your Occupy movement could ever begin to pass Congress: and the reason? Two words: The South."

This was a heavy-duty class lecture from Professor Oliver Neville, and we were both quiet for a few miles to digest the implications. Then Oliver seemed to decide something and asked me to hold the wheel. He was wearing one of those professorial tweedy coats like he was in a pub in Ireland, and as I steered us down the highway, and he was saying how in class he had always worn the same bow tie with Yale colors, he reached in his inside pocket, took out a little beaded grandma coin purse, reached in, and popped something squirrely-looking in his mouth.

He handed me the purse and said, "Shroom?"

I took the bag, and Neville added, "They're organic, fair trade ha ha ha, and locally grown by the same guy who sold me the malt and hops for the beer."

And with that, he handed me another home brew to wash down the mushrooms, which tasted like bits of warm tire. Soon I was outside the van and doing the backstroke alongside it, and even the blue apocalyptic gas flames of Newark had a certain undeniable exquisiteness, and when main man Neville the Professor let loose with some more Whitman:

And will there never be any more perfection than there is now,
Nor any more heaven and hell than there is now

I turned to lock my eyes to his blue oracular orbs with some gratitude, because until this moment, I would never have believed *that* for a second. Because my whole life was about fighting to change hell *into* heaven and making things *more* perfect in America for her citizens, not just the sociopathic 1% who had Justice Roberts on the Supreme Court of the land announcing like the Mad Hatter that corporations were people, and money was free speech, and that the Captains of Capitalism could strip the diapers off ten dead babies for a dime. But for that moment, near Newark, heading south to my destiny however obscure, I was freed from the furious prison of my own fiery passion for America, and all things were good.

And so, to thank Professor Neville for the beer, shrooms, and momentary relief from unbearable activistic urges, I said, quoting Whitman back, to let him know I digested that all was kosher thanks to the twinkling in us of death-grown psilocybins, "Clear and sweet is my soul, and clear and sweet is all that is not my soul."

My dear Neville brother nodded in deep cosmic affirmation and passed the grandma purse, and I sprinkled a few more shreds of marvelous mushrooms into my mouth as it glommered open like a baby bird's.

And then the night took a majestically weird turn, as the van was yanked off the highway, and after some scattered weavings through the bleak streets of industrial Camden, stuttered to a halt outside the giant iron gates of a cemetery filled with large antique granite monuments and obelisks glowing with the faint touch of a yellow moon.

"Are you ready?" he said finally, touching my cheek, his sunken, darkly humored eyes and thick beard suddenly giving him a look of a black Whitman.

"For what?" I said. As his hand on my cheek had broken through the shroom hallelujah and given me pause.

But Neville was already opening my door and aiding my stiff leg out of the van. He took me by the hand, told me with some merriment to close my eyes, and led me into this seemingly random cemetery in Camden. And soon enough—though my eyes had been wide open the whole way—he told me to look, and there before me, built into a small hillside, was a stone mausoleum about ten feet tall, with large carved letters across the top that read: WHITMAN.

Neville went up and pressed his hands against the face of the blue-gray granite, and as this seemed a good way to give homage to one of the most expansive of American souls, I went up and pressed my cheek to the cold stone, too.

"Walt designed it himself," said Neville, kissing the stone a few times. To be honest, it looked like he was going to cry, and he turned his head away from me.

Neville went silent, and I closed my eyes and tried to have a conversation with Walt about why more Americans couldn't chill on all their greedy doings and *loaf* more like him; then I felt Neville behind me, and he was breathing heavily on my ear and whispering, "Stop this day and night with me and you shall possess the origin of all poems," and pressing me hard against the granite. And I'll say right up front I'm not gay—and even more sure about that *now*—so it is a little weird I let Professor Neville undo my belt, yank my pants down, and do me in the ass up against Walt's mausoleum. But I just absolutely didn't care anymore what happened to my body in this world, and he was clearly in a slathering need, and I wanted to let him slake his thirst, so that we could head south, bonded by this sacred—but really sort of painful—

Greek-style brotherhood. And I admit he got to me with that line from Whitman, the one about how I might *possess the origin of all poems* if I let him do his backdoor thing, and that seemed like a fair trade.

Things might have been sort of OK—other than for my poor ass—if Professor Neville hadn't started to pant out as he galloped against me toward the finish line. He was reciting fast and furious:

> My lovers . . . suffocate me!
> Crowding my lips . . . and thick in the pores of my skin . . . coming naked to me at night . . .
> Calling my . . . name . . . from . . . flowerbeds . . .

Maybe it was the loud reciting of Whitman that pushed his big heart into the fibrillation zone. I know that running while singing is a whole lot more tiring than just grimly running. But it was right at that word *flowerbeds*, which he just bazoomed out like a true Neville Brother of New Orleans, that he gave a final wicked thrust and then yanked out of me and dropped backwards to the grass.

So I have taken the EMT class three times in my life (rescuing people in an emergency situation has always attracted me), but failed each time due to a certain inability to sit still in a classroom, but I do think I can diagnose *death*. And despite ten minutes of CPR, my comrade Professor Neville of Cornell was stone dead on his back, his corduroys at his knees, his final erection strangely still saluting the grave of Walt Whitman.

There wasn't a lot of time to say the proper words, because I saw red and blue spangling off the highest tombstones. So I gave Neville a kiss on his full open lips, slipped the van keys and wallet from his pocket, and made a sacred vow to him, with my hand over his silent heart. Then I leapt an iron railing like the hurdler I was in high school and flew like a ghost down a row of tombstones. Glancing back, I could see the Camden police were now at Whitman's grave, and then they started to shout in heavy cop voices, and the flashlight beams played all over the graveyard, and I dove to the lawn, changed direction, and crawled toward the road.

I hid behind a tombstone topped with the weeping angel of a Miss Gladys Willowell, who lived only eighteen years and died in 1872. Then I ran hunched over toward the van, as I knew soon the cemetery would be crawling with cops, and someone would have a brainstorm and run back for the vehicle.

I figured it was the van that had tipped the cops off that some Whitman-worshipping hippies were probably dropping acid at Walt's granite grave. I expected not to make such a clean getaway, but I just drove away—casually and without incident—and not badly for someone still seeing colored comet tails from lights—and was soon back on the interstate heading south to my manifest destiny.

It will come as no surprise that I was a little rattled in my soul at this moment in my life. So I tried to uncap a home brew with my teeth, but I chipped a molar and cut my lip. Blood drops were speckling my Occupy T-shirt, and it looked scarily symbolic. I just gave up and let my ripped lip hang and slowly drip blood as I drove, and kept seeing my friend Professor Neville dead on his back in the cemetery, and as I crossed into Delaware, started cogitating in an obsessively circular way on how my friend Neville had said there was a revolution coming in America, and all it needed was a spark.

Up ahead emerged a huge brightly lit airplane hangar of a welcome center, and my hands turned the wheel, and I was barreling off the highway. The van was dangerously low on biodiesel, so I proceeded to the lonely end of the parking lot, scrambled up on the roof, took down a big blue jug of French fry grease, and filled up the van. But as I was filling, my head got dizzy, and I was deeply aware that I was twenty-eight, that a rare kind of Whitman-man had just had sex with me and died, that Occupy was over for me, that America had frozen into an oligarchy, and that the sound of hundreds of global warming machines zooming by out there on the dark interstate was the sound of my heart sizzling like it had been ripped out and tossed on a red-hot engine. For a moment I thought of pulling the blue jug out of the van, pouring the fry oil over my head, and putting my finger in the van's cigarette lighter.

That chilled me: that I was totally serious about turning myself into a human tiki torch. It got me into the van, where with shaking hands I took another sprinkle of mushrooms from the grandma purse, opened a beer (this time on the door of the van), and chugged it down. Then I scorched out the on-ramp with the pedal to the floor. I sensed that some fanged grief or something was crouched in the back of the van, and about ten miles down the road, just after a sign that said sixty miles to Washington, DC, it viciously grabbed me around the neck from behind. Out of the blue I was just choking on sobs—I hadn't cried since I was a kid, it was a shock—and it was such a violent gagging and heaving that I could barely see the road, and I had the feeling I was drowning in black tears. But I found a way to fight back and rescue myself, and it was this: I started to *scream*. I glanced in the rearview mirror, and I looked just like that famous painting by Edvard Munch of the dude squeezing his head at the ears and letting out a sonic howl that melted his face.

So for the next thirty miles I screamed in the dark van of a dead man. I didn't scream all the thirty miles, sometimes I chilled and obsessively listed my political grievances as a member of the 99%, because it was just good to hear my own voice in the empty van, but my voice was pretty corroded from all the violent screaming, like someone had roughed up my vocal cords with a dental drill. Then I'd go back to my jungle screaming, and once it got so bad and I was weeping so brutally I had to pull off the road, and just after the van came to a halt I swear I heard a voice talk out loud to me. And it wasn't just any voice, it was Professor Neville's, and he said just as he did at Whitman's grave, *You shall possess the origin of all poems.*

There was some peace after Professor Neville spoke to me. I drove blindly onward, kind of slumped and hanging on to the steering wheel like it was a rescue ring thrown to a drowning man. The next time I was aware of a state, I was in West Virginia, and it was like the good green van had driven me to my final destination, like I was now just a passenger. There was an awakening moment when I remembered from junior-high-school geography, that here three states came together where the Susquehanna River merged with the Potomac. And then it hit me like a silver hammer between the eyes what was at that union of rivers. Two words: Harpers Ferry.

It was still night when I parked behind some three-story Victorian building right smack in the historic town. I just sat there sucking down Professor Neville's home brews and chewing on the dregs of the mushrooms. Then, when dawn came, I rustled around for a paper and a pen to write a letter to my sister Margaret, and luckily the professor man had a van full of notepads, but he also had lots of books, and the first one I put my hands on was about old John Brown.

The author of this biography wasn't a huge fan of JB. He compared him to Timothy McVeigh and Osama bin Laden, said he was "America's First Terrorist," painted it on dark about how he was "tortured by dreams of righteous godly violence" and in general was fanatical, monomaniacal, murderous, an evil zealot, psychotic and . . . *stubborn.* Maybe it was the last of the mushrooms, but after he'd slapped JB as the twin brother of the Antichrist, the tack-on of that squishy word stubborn just totally cracked me up, and I was laughing so hard tears were rolling down my cheeks.

It was in this strange mood of thunder-headed mania that I got out of the van with a lighter in my pocket. Then I climbed up and took down one of the blue containers of biodiesel, and started down Shenandoah Street. John Brown had come here expecting 4,500 righteous warriors to follow him into history's book of glory, but in the end had only twenty-one dudes, one of whom had the excellent name Dangerfield Newby. As I hobbled along the antique street with my canister of biodiesel it felt like it was 1859, and I remember saying out loud, "Call me Dangerfield," and sort of chuckling.

And then I was at the Fire House, the very building where John Brown and his small band had lit the fuse that exploded in the Civil War and the end of slavery. I got down on my knees and bowed my head—not that I am religious—but it seemed like the appropriate thing to do in honor of JB.

There was a scaffold set up at the back of the fire house for some restoration work. It seemed like a sign to me. Blue canister in hand, I climbed the silver scaffold, and scrambled on my hands and knees up the roof of American history until I stood next to a small, pretty glass cupola.

And there I stood as dawn arose over Harpers Ferry. It was as if the glorious souls of John Brown and his twenty-one sacrificial heroes funneled upward into the cupola, and as the sun rose, a fiery light reflected off the ancient panes of glass, and I stood bathed in a golden glow. I knew I wasn't coming down off the roof of the Fire House, and that I had finally found a way to use my 180 useless pounds of flesh for *good*.

It wasn't until the first tour came to the Fire House with a National Park ranger that some child looked up and spotted me. Then things moved quickly. The ranger called on her radio for backup, and I unscrewed the top of the blue canister, straddled the rooftop with a foot on both sides, raised the canister over my head, and *glug-glug-glugged* that grease over my body for what seemed like five minutes. It actually didn't smell like French fries, but more like onion rings.

I dropped the blue canister, and it skittered down the roof. The crowd jumped back as if it was going to explode. I fished in my pocket and took out the gold lighter, held it aloft. Soon there were firemen and cops on the scaffold. I remained silent. There were hundreds of people down below now, and TV cameras were set up, and SWAT team guys with their rifles pointed at me from the rooftops of the antique buildings.

I knew it was time to flick the lighter held aloft in my right hand. But then I remembered some words I had just read in the van by John Brown, and I decided a good quotation might help people to get that I was more than a crazy fool. So I recited loudly in my raspy, broken voice: *"Had I acted on behalf of the rich, the powerful, the so-called great, or their friends and family, you would have deemed me worthy of reward. But to have acted on behalf of the poor was not wrong but right."*

With that I placed the lighter to my heart, raised my eyes to the clouds above for the final time, and flicked my thumb. There was a roar from the crowd, and I looked down at the lighter and flicked again. Then I flicked it again, and again, and again.

THE HOT WAR

My daughter fell through the ice in her ninth year. A crack opened and ate her up, her puffy red coat sinking into the black water as I watched, her new CCM hockey stick spinning like a compass needle. This was in our backyard pond. I pushed forward with my palms and slid into the water and kicked straight down. The iron stem of a mushroom anchor nailed me between the eyes, and I rolled over on my back and looked up at the hole in the ice, the murky circle of light. My fingers touched her drifting hair, and I clenched my fist and swam crazily for the surface. Somehow I shoveled her limp body up and out. I was newly divorced. She was spending Christmas with me in Montana. There was no one else.

Halogens bathed the scene in a razor light. My great-grandfather had built the farmhouse and dug the pond, and we Addisons had skated safely here in December for sixty years. There was plenty of ice. There was no way it cracked but it cracked. I stumbled in my hockey skates across the snow with Chloe in my arms. Ten miles out of Whitefish in the woods, I wasn't waiting for an ambulance. She had a wavering pulse at her carotid, and I gave her mouth-to-mouth with her head in my lap while bombing at eighty over the frozen washboard roads. I had never kissed her on the lips. Her eyes were wide open and dilated. She gagged up a pink, frothy spittle, and I was so excited I sideswiped a snowbank. On impact, she slid to the floor of the passenger seat. There was nothing to do but pull her up by her hair and keep driving and pumping her full of breath.

At the hospital they put her on a mechanical ventilator and kicked me out of the ER. I swiped a mask and gown and slipped back in with a surgeon and his nurses. Her heart stopped; they cut off the rest of her nightgown—it was a last skate before hot chocolate and bedtime—and hit her with the paddles. Her stomach was all watermeloned out. That morning the *I Ching* had said: *You are found at the bottom of a dirty well.*

Up until the divorce six months earlier, Chloe and I had spent most of our days together. She was homeschooled because once I retired at thirty after selling an app, all I wanted to do was be with her and help her enjoy every moment of childhood. It wasn't so much a *tempus fugit* thing, but more that I was pretty sure the world was heading for an eco-apocalypse in her lifetime and her adulthood would suck fried eggs.

Her bluish lips quivered, and she said in her arch little voice, "Vic!" She always called me by my first name, she never gave it up to me as a father. I mean, she always saw us as equals. She believed in kid rights and wrote to President Obama about the voting age. She knew she was in vitro. I made her laugh because I could mimic people pretty well and glue-gun paperclips into an Eiffel Tower. She went topless at the pond in summer because her boy cousins did. At nine she finally learned to read by listening to *Harry Potter* tapes. She was dyslexic like me but could memorize a poem on first hearing it. She thought dancing was running in place like your feet were on fire, and she'd have this sweet, earnest look on her face. She killed me with her dancing.

"Chloe-monster!" I screamed from behind my mask.

Everyone looked at me. I looked at my daughter's lips.

"She said my name!" I yelled, slapping a nurse on the back. "She said, 'Vic!' That's me! I'm Vic! She's Chloe! Together we're the Chloe-vics, Lords of Light!"

The nurse spoke briefly into a phone and turned back to the heart monitor. Everyone was concentrating. Gloved hands circled over her body like bats. Another nurse said, "Sixty-two degrees." She was such a shriveled baby bird of a girl. You'd think that we never—that *I* never—fed her, but she was a vegetarian from the age of four. Chickens in a cage made her furious, as did smokestacks. Her first word was *agua*.

She pointed at a glass of water and said, "*Agua!*" though we don't speak Spanish and didn't have a TV. I recited *A Midsummer Night's Dream* to her in the crib, recalled from my actor days; and of Chloe it was true: *Though she be but little, she is fierce.*

Some orderlies showed up and surrounded me like a rugby scrum, then drove me out to the waiting room as I screamed, "There was plenty of ice! There was plenty of ice!" If you see people dying every day, you get used to fathers going crazy. And by the way, I was a really good dad: so good it destroyed my marriage; I loved Chloe much more than my wife. And my wife loved Chloe more than me. The last thing I heard was a saw as they cracked open her chest. The last thing I saw, fighting back to the circular window, was her little heart covered in tinfoil.

She was cremated two days later and her dust poured into a marble jar that my wife, Zoe, painted with violets, woodbine, and eglantine. At the funeral, I stood up with a drugged, rubbery tongue and tried to recite Oberon's lines about the sleeping fairy queen, Titania. I'd always put Chloe to bed with those lines:

> I know a bank where the wild thyme blows,
> Where oxlips and the nodding violet grows,
> Quite over-canopied with luscious woodbine,
> With sweet musk-roses and with eglantine.

I tried to explain that eglantine is a kind of rose bush, which Zoe and I had planted on the east side of the farmhouse the week we were married. I said Chloe liked to gather the petals and make them into flower water, as they do in Tunisia. She'd strip the bushes bare. I was quiet for a moment, looking at my hands, and then my best friend, Evan, walked me back to my seat. He said I'd been mumbling about the ice again.

Two days after the funeral I moved out to a cabin Evan had in Glacier National Park. He'd never mentioned it before. It was on the North Fork, in Big Prairie, and accessible in summers by an old Butte Oil Company road to Kintla Lake. In winters, however, the only ways in were by snowshoe, ski, or horseback. Snow was falling big and wet that morning as I rented a young gelding named White Calf from an outfit on the edge of the park and rode in. I stripped down to a T-shirt as the temperature rose to seventy-five degrees, the heavy flakes on the ground melting under my pissed-off gaze.

The cabin was well stocked if you liked canned cannellini beans and airplane shot-bottles of booze. Evan's family owned a company that supplied the airlines. There was dry hemlock firewood in the barn. I put White Calf in a stall and tossed him an old bale of hay, then commenced working through the bar. In the propane fridge I found—inexplicably—at least six bags of ice. Chloe loved to crunch ice. She'd order slushies without all the colored, poisonous goo and smash away with her premolars. I showed her how I could shatter two whole cubes at once, and she was working her way up to one the night she dropped through.

Another thing Evan had failed to mention was that he'd been screwing Zoe for years. Here's how I figured it out: Alone in the cabin, I got to thinking about a photo taken the day Chloe was born—one I'd staged so it looked like flowers were bursting out of her heart. To shake the image from my mind I drank a dozen midget bottles, but the booze wasn't working. So I popped a few pills a doctor friend had prescribed and banged my head on a cabinet until blood blinded my eyes. Then I stumbled to the barn to hug the horse. White Calf tolerated me for a while, until he flipped out and kicked the shit out of his stall. As he rampaged through the rest of the barn, I jumped into a neighboring stall, where apparently Evan dumped his recycling in the winter when the park road was closed. I sat there weeping and bleeding and sorting it out. I have this thing about organizing recycling into its components: paper, metal, plastic, and glass. It seems hopeful. Which is how I found three of my wife's credit card receipts, one going back years. I guess he'd tried to sanitize the place of her. So much for Zoe's trips to see her sister Ellen in Brooklyn. And then, piled up with the empty cans, I noticed a number of pieces of tinfoil squeezed into ragged silver balls. I don't know how I'd missed them. Chloe had always been into line drawings, lately working with indelible marker on sheets of tinfoil. Zoe thought they were a little obsessive, but I compared her lines to the abstract work of Paul Klee. I'd saved hundreds of them: every scrap stacked neatly under a stone on my desk. And there on the floor of the mangled barn, as I unraveled drawing after drawing, all I could see was the circular window in the ER, all I could see was my daughter's tinfoil heart.

It took some encouragement to get White Calf into the cabin. I led him to the doorway and pushed on his ass, and he gave a nasty kick that sent me rolling around the muddy yard, howling. When I finally looked up, he was in the kitchen. I dumped a few cans of beans on the table and sat in a spindle-back chair with a bag of ice on my sternum as he lapped up the mess, his teeth like yellowed piano keys. And then he squeezed out a tumbling, wet torrent of shit on Evan's antique Blackfoot Indian rug.

The horse looked mightily relieved, but I was only more inflamed. The temperature outside was dropping, so I threw a bunch of wood into the hearth, and soon a big fire was roaring and spitting. And as I stood in its ring of heat, Puck's words popped into my head:

> Not a mouse
> Shall disturb this hallow'd house.

Not a mouse, but maybe a stallion of fifteen hands. White Calf neighed and kicked his foreleg in a dyspeptic way. The beans didn't seem to be sitting well. I love animals, as much as Chloe did, but suddenly I was running at him with a vintage snowshoe I ripped from the wall. I swatted him across the flank, and he reared and smashed through the walnut coffee table. And as he turned his bright, frightened eyes on me, I got another idea.

In high school I knew a guy name Artie Henson who worked summers as a heifer inseminator. He squirted bull sperm into lady cows. He'd told me a bit about animal organs, so I reached out and gave that young horse's cock a quick tug. He sprang forward on his forelegs, raised up his back legs, and completely annihilated the living room wall. The force knocked me to the floor, and I guess White Calf then charged me, knocking me out cold with a hoof to the skull. I deserved it.

ໄຊ ໄຊ

When I came to, the fire was glowing cinders, and the house smelled like horseshit and vomit. It appeared the vomit was mine. I took a double dose of narcotics and sipped a shot on ice, and none of it softened the banging in my head.

I lay there for another hour, or perhaps three, until I realized I was actually worried about myself. And then some lines from Theseus dropped into my thinking:

> Merry and tragical! Tedious and brief!
> That is, hot ice and wondrous strange snow.

The room grew warmer, and I struggled to my feet. White Calf was in the kitchen with his head in the fridge, probably looking for something to eat. I pushed past him and found a big cookie tin in the back filled with trail mix, heavy on the M&M's. A commemorative saddle hung above the mantel, and I pulled it down and slipped it over the horse's back. With shaking hands I filled the saddlebags with the trail mix, a few dozen bottles of booze, and a raised topographical map of the park that I took from the bedroom wall and cut to fit. I rolled up a bunch of blankets and tied them on the back of the saddle. All the while, the earworm continued to whisper: *Hot ice and wondrous strange snow.*

I led White Calf out the cabin doors—they were painted with the flag of Montana which had to be the ugliest flag in the world—and was slapped by the heat, which must have been pushing eighty. There were crazy shimmers of chlorophyll in the yellow grass. The horse stomped his feet, at first too freaked to leave the barn. A flock of birds passed overhead, and they seemed to be flying backward. I mounted White Calf, rubbed his flank, and asked his forgiveness. And with that, we set off.

ໄຊ ໄຊ

There were glaciers still in Glacier National Park—25 remained of the

150 that had existed here in the mid-nineteenth century. But in less than a decade they'd all be gone. At that point I hadn't exactly connected my hunger to stand on a melting glacier with anything. I was just moving forward, trying to keep my rapidly disintegrating self together for a few more clip-clops.

As White Calf bumped along the muddy road, I pulled the map from the saddlebag. I'd set my sights on Kintla Glacier, the closest one, about eight miles on. The problem was I couldn't see too well: My vision was blurry. I'd been sipping from the bottles every time I thought of Chloe; I might have swallowed a few more pills, too. Or maybe White Calf had done some serious damage when he kicked me in the head. Chloe and I used to build enormous igloos in the backyard. Our technique was to pile the snow in a giant heap, then dig out the interior. We'd make several and connect them with tunnels. Spatulas were the tool of choice. Chloe liked to carve the walls so thin they turned blue from the refracted light. Sometimes we'd get blankets and books and sleeping bags and camp out for a night. She'd always end up in my bag, her hot little breaths warming my shoulder.

White Calf and I were trudging along under a clean sky on the closed North Fork Road. We'd turn east toward Bowman Creek, then inward to the glacier. I must have taken my shirt off; the sweat pouring down my body smelled like more booze. Yet I was only vaguely aware of all that, as I was still with Chloe in our perfect blue igloo, until I noticed the grizzly emerging from the brush—or until White Calf noticed the grizzly. The horse reared like in a Hollywood western, and I crashed abruptly to the earth. As I watched him fade into the landscape, the only sound was the warm piss running between my legs.

I woke in the bed of a jacked-up pickup, careening down the rutted road, slaloming wildly, my head rattling against the ski of an Arctic Cat ProCross snowmobile with an MSRA—Montana Snowmobile Racing Association—sticker on its flyscreen. It was late afternoon based on the shadows. I must have been out for five hours or so. I got up on my knees in a sort of cow position, and encountered a bright, angelic face grinning at me from the open window of the cab's open rear window. I recognized her immediately. Eloise Red Crow was what passed for a celebrity in these parts—a Blackfoot whose Pocahontas looks had led to a promising modeling career in Manhattan. But an attraction to pills, as well as more existential issues, had recently pulled her back to the reservation. Her hair was an almost ethereal white-blond, falling straight down on either side of sanguine lips. She opened her mouth to show me two pills and a gold tongue stud. In her crazy good cheer I saw something of a grown-up Chloe, and I was ready to accompany this truck to whatever constellation was its destination. Behind the wheel, the very large shoulders and ponytailed skull of Joe Bull Shoe, former heavyweight boxer, didn't trouble me yet.

A pothole dropped me flat to my chest, and it was then I realized I had no pants on. My brain wasn't firing on all synapses. Eloise Red Crow stuck her face in the little window to yell, "You pissed your pants," which didn't totally explain why they'd left me bare-assed in the back of the truck. Just as I was beginning to suspect some sort of revenge-on-the-white-man game, she reached out and ran her fingers through my hair, touched her cool palm to my cheek; and in her touch, some of the grief and anger drained from me—this calming was something I had never experienced with Zoe or anyone. My eyes had fallen closed by the time she drew her hand away, and when it returned she placed a pill on my tongue. By its metallic taste I knew it wasn't Demerol. We hit another pothole and swerved again, flopping me on my back, and I finally found my pants—they were tied by my belt to the silver roll bar, snapping like a jean flag.

Splayed there in the rocking bed, mostly exposed, I felt like an animal. So I stood and grabbed for my pants, but missed and caught the roll bar, where I hung on for a bit, enjoying the spruce trees hurtling past and the strangely warm wind in my face. I glanced down to discover Eloise's delicate hand locked around my cock. She thought that was the funniest thing, and didn't let go; but if there was a joke I'm pretty sure Joe Bull didn't get it. Still, I just decided to go with it—there wasn't a lot of choice—and with her warming hand, and the jiggling truck, I rose up like a totem pole.

My mind was soaring—or perhaps her pill was simply kicking in— and I lifted my chin to the gathering clouds above and recited:

Over hill, over dale,
Thorough bush, thorough brier,
Over park, over pale,
Thorough flood, thorough fire,
I do wander everywhere . . .

My ability to care was toasted, and my *everywhere* was in the hands of two drugged and drunk Blackfeet. The truck jounced around a corner and skidded to a stop in the parking lot of a visitor center. The tailgate crashed down, and Joe Bull jumped in with his feet together: an impressive display—you have to be in superior shape to do that sort of shit. He was wearing black jeans and a Gold's Gym wife-beater, and stomping around in expensive Baffin Eiger snowmobile boots. I belly-rolled over the side of the truck to get the hell out of his furious way. I tried to stick the landing, but the parking lot was rippled and I ended up on my ass. Joe Bull hurled my pants at me, then revved his giant snowmobile and launched it down a metal ramp to the pavement.

"You're a sweet-faced man," Eloise Red Crow said, looking down at me. She bit the tip off an icicle she had snapped off one of those National Park trailhead signs, and extended a hand to help me up. She had a ruby ring on her middle finger that flickered with light. Eloise Red Crow was a good five inches taller than me. She had a small crescent-moon scar below her right eye, and in her chin a crater of a dimple. Her teeth were extraterrestrial white, her eyes an unusual glacial blue. As if reading my mind, she pointed with the icicle to the trailhead to the glacier. On his snowmobile, Joe Bull was ripping tight doughnuts in the parking lot.

He shuddered to a halt, and she slid on behind him and patted the seat behind her, saying, "Let's go see the hot ice and wondrous strange snow." Drugged and drunk and despairing as I was, there was a message in this synchronicity. And I was in deep need of a message.

We rocketed through a narrow alley of huge red cedars, the engine so loud I had to lean forward and squeeze my lips to Eloise Red Crow's little ear to yell questions like, "How did you know the wondrous-snow line?" She yelled back, "I played Titania Off-Off-Broadway last year!" She kissed me just as Joe Bull blasted through a snowbank, and our faces smashed hard together. I put my hand to my nose and it came away bloody. She grinned at the sight, baring red-speckled teeth. And then Joe Bull put the hammer down.

Moments later we broke out of the trees and slid onto the wide-open expanse of St. Mary Lake. Eloise Red Crow turned—her upper lip still dripping blood—and yelled, "We're almost there!" The snowmobile dropped a gear, and Joe Bull raised up into a squat and opened the throttle. The screaming motor assaulted the gigantic primal emptiness.

We burned miles across the lake, tearing through a few inches of slush. Eloise Red Crow pointed to Otokomi and Red Eagle Mountains, and each time she spoke her warm, wind-carried blood sprayed my face. And it was against the warmth of her blood that I suddenly realized the temperature was tumbling fast. A black cloudbank was descending like a UFO from up in Logan Pass. The slush was going rigid beneath us.

Everything started when my daughter fell through warming ice in the backyard, and it ended when Joe Bull hit freezing ice in the middle of St. Mary Lake. The snowmobile hung sideways for a delicate moment. Then Joe Bull ripped it back too hard and time snapped and we cranked over. All I can imagine is he refused to let go; when the big machine flipped, it landed on him—and broke his neck. My hands left Eloise Red Crow's warm back and I hit the ice in a swan dive, then skidded for what seemed like a half mile.

☞ ☜

Giant snowflakes were melting on my face, and a brisk wind wrestled the cedars along the lakeshore. I raised my head. I saw the ruined and smoking snowmobile, and Joe Bull's paper-clipped body, but no sign of Eloise Red Crow. Then trembling fingers brushed my cheek. I reached up and touched her hair. I could feel her weeping.

The weeping got me to my knees, every part of me in eye-squinting pain. I bent over Eloise. Her collarbone was pushing unnaturally against her skin, as if trying to break through, and her knee was wrecked. I looked down the long, empty lake; and the distance disappeared before my eyes, lost in dark shadows and the swirling snow. We were at the bottom of a dirty well.

I scooped her up and stumbled to a tiny, rocky island five hundred feet away. Eloise's voice was cracking and small as she told me this had been the destination all along: Wild Goose Island. The snow was thicker, spun by the wind into ghostly shapes. Eloise said the island had a legend. Two lovers from tribes at war were left there to say good-bye before they were to be separated forever. But the Great Spirit saw the depth of their love. He turned them into geese, and together they flew away.

On the lee side of the island, I kicked and scraped out a shallow bowl in the snow and placed Eloise in it. She was shivering violently. I gathered branches of lodgepole pines and built a tepee over her, then crawled in, too; she buried her face in my neck. She said she was thirsty, so I put snow in her mouth. As I held her in my arms, the blizzard intensified—soon we were entombed. She said, "It hurts so much," and drifted off to sleep.

Hours passed in the darkness, and then a single drop of water fell on my forehead, followed by more drops. I punched my hand through the wall of our igloo, and it was fucking warm as summer again. Eloise was breathing dreamily beside me.

I crawled out and stood under a crystalline night sky. Everything was rapidly melting all around. Water is alive. I am water. It hurts so much. I killed my daughter. I broke the ice.

OPPENHEIMER BEACH

"Get off your iPad," Hugh Copley said. He was lying in a hammock tied between two palm trees. The hammock—or at least *a* hammock—had been there forever, as the hooks were nearly swallowed by the elephant bark of the palms. He twisted angrily, trying to get the canvas to swing. He had spent the night in this sling, and the no-see-ums at dawn had savaged his face and neck. The sheet in which he had wrapped himself like a mummy lay crumpled on the sandy ground. He took a hit off the last of three joints the local kid had slipped into his hand as they checked into the cottage the night before. Raising his head, he pointed a long arm, with a gesture that seemed too fluid, toward the screened window. "I know you're on the thing," he said. "There better not be wifi on the beach, or we're for Borneo. Fuck Steve Jobs. The guy is the Antichrist." A blond head popped up at the screen. The boy was standing with his legs spread on a waterbed—an odd touch for a tropical cottage—and because he was alternately pressing his feet down, he floated unnaturally in the window. "Why do you think I brought you people to paradise?" The boy was still in the same red plaid pants he always wore, white sneakers without a spot, a black T-shirt that tried to hide his weight and a chest that was almost girlish. Around his neck were two gold chains—Hugh had under duress given him one for Christmas a few days earlier, though his real gift to his son was his own first Leica, and enough film for the next three to six months of their trip.

"Magnus, did you hear me?"

Magnus was still framed in the window, but now his eyes were focused downward, and his shoulders twitched as his fingers worked their magic on the computer game he had been playing since the roosters had awoken him. He raised his eyes once or twice to his father in the hammock a dozen feet away. Hugh Copley was a war photographer and his work had been in *The New York Times* and *National Geographic*: stories on Myanmar, Durban, Kabul, and Grenada. In Kabul he had been kidnapped for twelve hours. He had been away on assignment for half his son's life. He gave a command well, he felt, and was always surprised his son didn't pay the least attention. He lowered his voice an octave. "Magnus. Put it down and come out here. At least step onto the porch and bring me a beer."

Magnus stopped surfing the waterbed, clenched the iPad to his chest like a shield, and gazed out through the pixilating screen. His milky-green eyes were his most interesting feature—they were set very wide, but too large for his face by two degrees, and hooded. They also tilted upward, which gave them an eerie feline, slightly—(Hugh felt bad that he saw this in them)—otherworldly, or to be more specific, alien aspect. His face, his eyes, his blond spiky hair: he was, like his Oslo-born mother, arrestingly good-looking despite his weight, but since Hugh had returned from Kabul, his son's evaluative gaze had kept him up at night.

"I simply want you to come outside," Hugh said.

"Stay where you are, my Magnus," said his wife, Alfhild, whose voice was strained, as she was levitating in the *kakasana*, or crow, yoga position. "You are not his flight attendant." This was a reference to the six beers he had ordered on the JetBlue flight down to the Virgin Islands from LaGuardia. By combining them with two Zoloft, he had achieved a perfectly numbed state that made the grind of the landing gear a painful psychic shock. Alfhild was looking at her son from the terracotta tiled floor, her short white-blond bangs framing her raised open face, the nine fingers (she had lost her left pinky to frostbite as a girl Telemarking in the fjord region) elevating her body straining, splayed, and bloodless. "You can stay in this room all day," she said, and gasped for a moment for breath as she held her pose. "Play your silly games."

"The elf-warrior speaks," said Hugh, in a Norwegian accent. "I should have married your friend Abigael. You can't go wrong with a name that means 'father rejoices.' I pay four hundred dollars a night for us to be here on this famous beach to kick off our '2009 End of the World Tour,' and I ask my son to step outside and at least touch a damn coconut or something on the very first morning, and you tell him to stay inside and play computer games. Is that helpful?"

"If a ten-year-old boy, whose father precipitously snatched him from his excellent school where he was getting good grades, because his father has a midlife crisis, wants to play computer games," Alfhild said, blinking with strain in the final moments of her pose. "I say let him."

"Sometimes, Alfhild," Hugh said. "I've wanted to put a machete through your pretty and pragmatic head like it was a ripe coconut."

"The machete is new."

Hugh fought his way out of the hammock and stretched, went to the small fridge on the back of the porch, took out a Corona, and waved it at the Caribbean Sea, the electric blue broken by a regimental curtain of palms a few dozen feet away. "You still don't get it," he began.

"I get that you have foolishly burned all your bridges and given up your photojournalism career," said Alfhild, as she lay recovering in *savasana*, the corpse position. Exhaling deeply, she crossed her arms across her breasts. "And I get that in six months or less, having completed this forced end-of-the-world-let-our-child-see-it-for-the-last-time odyssey, we'll return completely broke to New York, Magnus will be a year behind in his studies, we will probably divorce, and I will find a wealthy new lover, younger perhaps and more limber, who likes to play computer games with my son, and doesn't walk around drowning in guilt at being simply—"

"Enough," said Hugh, theatrically draining the beer, and reaching in the fridge for another. This time he pulled out a Red Stripe.

As he twisted the beer open with his teeth, Magnus emerged, sat on the top step, and pointed to his iPad. "I'm downloading just as fast as New York," he said slowly. "And it's routing locally, so I'm not using up any of my contract minutes." His voice was still unusually high-pitched. He looked at his father with almost rapture. "I was worried . . . it said I'd burn up contract minutes down here like they were on fire."

"I'll light a fire under you, Magster, if you don't turn that thing off," his father said. He drank half the beer. "Put it in your suitcase, and try and make it all the way down to the beach or something this morning." He stood on his toes to see his naked wife, who was now upside down, using her head and elbows for support, and then studied his son's face. "You look like a ghost. When was the last time you even walked outside?"

"I'll check," Magnus said. He put the iPad on his knees, and his fingers flicked across the screen. "I have an app that keeps track of where I've been. And if I want to know when I was *outside*—since I got the iPad at Christmas—I can just ask. Wait . . . Wait . . . Wait . . . Okay, I have been outside of a structure eight percent of the time, although I don't know what the app thinks of time in an airplane. Alfhild can access this application and see where I am at any moment. Alfhild, go on your laptop like I showed you and touch 'find Magnus' and tell Hugh where I am right now . . ."

"Magnus," Alfhild said, sounding strained. "Let mummy finish her yoga, then I promise to find you on the laptop."

"Okay," Magnus said, without raising his eyes. "Hey, the app seems to know I am 'outside' right now. It just changed the figure to nine percent. That's amazing. Because I'm just outside the screen door, about three feet from being 'inside.' How can it know that unless the GPS is a lot more accurate than they say? Or maybe the iPad is using sensory data, like the kind of light. Indoor light from bulbs is at a total different frequency than the stuff from the sun. But maybe this cottage isn't even a known structure? If so, all the time I spend here would count as 'outside.' But in that case I have been 'outside' since we came last night, and I must have been at like two percent or even one percent for 'outside' time before. Wait a minute, I can check my percentage at the time we got on the plane in New York."

"Hugh?" said Alfhild. "Did I hear you just crack another beer?"

"Ask Magnus," Hugh said. "He has an app that keeps track of his father's suicidal despair."

Magnus looked up earnestly at his father. "I can tell you your blood alcohol level. People use the app so they don't get a DWI." He stepped off the porch and took the empty Corona bottle, pointed his iPad at it and took a photo, then took a photo of the empty Red Stripe bottle. "That's 4.5 percent alcohol for the Corona, 4.2 percent for the Red Stripe. Both are twelve-ounce beers. You've had two Red Stripes and one Corona, and you started drinking with the first rooster, which was at 6:12 this morning, and it is now 7:19, which is an elapsed time of sixty-seven minutes. You are six feet three inches tall. What's your present body weight, Hugh? Have you gained back the weight you lost in Kabul?"

"One hundred ninety-two," Hugh said. He coughed as he pulled on the end of his joint. "I'm down thirty pounds and counting. No worries. It's the new Gandhi-me. If anyone sees that local kid today, let me know. I'm clearly going to need some more agricultural product. Is there an application for local child drug dealers, Magnus?"

"That's enough, Hugh." Alfhild pushed open the screen door and stepped onto the porch in a bright-yellow sarong. She pointed a finger at Hugh. "Don't punish my son because he doesn't share your new-found belief in nature as some sort of nasty god who demands we weep and gnash our teeth every time we use an electrical outlet."

"I doubt if it can legally find drug dealers," Magnus said. "But it can identify plants. I'll show you." He suddenly jumped off the porch, walked four steps toward a palm, and then slumped to the ground clutching his foot. He closed his eyes and rocked and said, "I think I stepped on some kind of sticky thorny thing." Alfhild ran over and held his foot, pulled out the thorn, and told him to go inside and get his Crocs.

"He's in a prison," Hugh said, shaking his head. "I can't explain it to you." He walked over and tried to touch his wife's back with his fingers, but she shrugged and went into the cottage. Hugh raised his voice and said, "I'll quit drinking and smoking cold turkey if you can get him to quit with the technology. But you'll have to help us both with our withdrawal symptoms. His will probably be worse."

"I am this close," Alfhild said from inside, "to taking Magnus back home, putting him back in his wonderful school, and pulling the plug on this madness."

Magnus came outside in his yellow Crocs. He was walking carefully. "I am going to identify something in the outside," he said over his shoulder to Alfhild. "To show Hugh."

"Magnus. If you go to the beach I want sunscreen on you."

"I think he'll be surprised," Magnus said, now talking lightly to himself, as if Hugh was not a few feet away. "If he sees what it can do out here in his nature, maybe he'll try it, and we can use it together on our trip. He just needs to see it work on what he likes, like a local tree or unusual bird or something—"

"Magnus," Alfhild said. "I'm going to look for you on the laptop now. Would you like that?"

"I could start with something easy," Magnus continued. "Like a coconut. I'll just take a photo of one, and it will tell me all about it. I think Hugh would like that, because even though he knows about coconuts, there are probably lots of facts about them he doesn't know. I could quiz Hugh, just to show—"

"Magnus," said Alfhild excitedly. "It works, Magnus. I have located you. I see you right here."

Magnus was busy leaning over and taking a photo of a coconut. "There," he said. "Soon we will know a million things about this coconut."

"Magnus," said Alfhild. "Walk fifty feet to the edge of the jungle. I want to see if you move."

"OK," said Magnus, who walked while scrolling. "Then I want to show Hugh all the facts about coconuts. There are even educational videos about the life cycles of palm trees."

Hugh was sitting on the back step looking at his beer. "He's fucked," he said to Alfhild inside. "We're all totally fucked."

"Give it a break," Alfhild said. "Why don't you go for a nice swim and cool off?"

"Alright, I'll go to the beach. But I want that thing put away. I want it put in a suitcase, or I am going to see what a coconut dropped from the roof of this cottage does to the screen."

Hugh yanked down his wraparound shades, jumped onto the beach from between two palm trees, studied his large feet on the hot sand, dashed toward an incoming wave, and stood as his feet were swallowed by the rushing water and sank deep into the soft sand. He looked down at his two white amputated peg legs and laughed. He raised his head, took a deep breath, and studied a small black island sloop with a bright-yellow bootstrap and sun-faded maroon sails as it skated rail down around the rocky point and snapped about in a brisk breeze to head into the bay. A West Indian man with Rastafarian hair to his waist saluted with a raised palm, and the sloop, in the tranquil blue bay bristling with the morning sun, hesitatingly nosed about again before the dark reef, and luffed toward Hawksnest Beach, beyond the outcropping of rocks at the end of his beach. There were a dozen tourists over there on Hawksnest, but Hugh's beach was empty of tourists, and he closed his eyes and raised his hands and opened his palms to the sun. He had seen this posture once on ancient Egyptian sculptures, and had adopted this salute whenever he arose with open sky available. He waited until his palms were warm, and when he opened his eyes, watched three pelicans arc down and smash together into a school of skittering minnows.

The cottage's designated chairs, wood and striped green, were sunk in the virgin sand, left below the tide line by the last guests. He dropped heavily into a chair. He closed his eyes for ten minutes, the sun cooking his nose, where he had a melanoma removed the year before. He touched the slight divot between his eyes, looked at his long, heavily boned white legs, and then studied his wedding ring, looking at a bright diamond sparkle on the gold that came and went as he adjusted the angle of his finger. Then he stood and walked back up to the shoreline, and returned with a notebook and a pen he had left on a rock.

September 12, 2009
Oppenheimer Beach, St. John

Magnus does not know how to play outside? He literally doesn't know "play" exists. It is like "snow" to the Masai.

The frankincense trees of Ethiopia will be extinct in a few years from global warming, cattle grazing, and invasive species. If Jesus came back, he'd get myrrh and gold, and I'm doubtful about myrrh, too. If Magnus ever wants to know what F trees looked like, he could look at my pictures at home.

Magnus does not know "nature" exists, except as he sees it as an abstraction on a screen.

If Magnus has no sense of "nature" as a living thing of dirt under the nails, can he have a sense of "Magnus" as a living, sensory, fleshy animal?

For Christmas I gave Magnus my photo of a Malagasy giant rat of Madagascar jumping three feet in the air. I told him we will try to see a real one on this trip, if there are any left. We will have to sit out all night. Alfhild said it was a very weird gift, but I thought a giant rat in midair was very cool for a boy.

I slept in my bathing suit when we went to the beach. All my friends did the same. We didn't spend five minutes in the house all day unless we were sick enough to die. The only time we were happy was when we were in the waves or rolling down the dunes. We explored for miles and came home with skin like scorched paper. No parent ever knew where we were: We had perfect freedom. This is over for children.

The only time Magnus is with a gang of kids outside is on a poisoned soccer field for an hour of Nazi ball chasing.

I find to my surprise I am a freak. Jesus said give up all you have and follow me. It is that sort of feeling. A wartime feeling. Jesus should have spent all his time on the beauty of the lilies in the valley.

There is just enough time for this last trip. Maybe it would be kind to put him gently to sleep when this trip is over with an opium cocktail. Alfhild would kill me. I would go happily with my son.

I think it was over for me when I saw forty-eight leopard skins for sale in Kabul right after I was thrown from the car and freed. I understood at once.

I don't think Magnus can "feel" beauty. There is something missing. A clear blue sky is an emotion, not a fact.

Magnus dreamed about animals as a boy. And then he stopped. Imagination comes from the soil; without dirty feet and freedom to wander as a child, I wonder if there can be imagination in the adult?

Alfhild says Magnus is stressed, anxious, and depressed because his grades are not good enough for a good college. She wants him to have tutoring after school and this summer. I'd die first.

I loved the ocean and the sand dunes as a boy, and then later I learned all about marine biology and the flora and fauna of Cape Cod. The love and tactile experience came first, and the hunger was there to learn later about the things I loved. I loved to look at things as a boy, and that led me to want to capture what I saw, and that led me to study the laws of photography.

In Manaus, Brazil—Manaus means "mother of the gods"—I took photos of tiny coffins made just for children, and that night I decided on this trip for Magnus.

Hugh was no longer alone on the beach. There was a West Indian boy climbing a coconut tree behind him. The sea had eroded around the root ball of the palm tree during the last hurricane, and now it leaned almost sideways. The boy, a muscular, shirtless twelve-year-old, had a head full of Rastafarian hair and wore baggy red swimming trunks. Crouched like a surfer, he was skillfully walking up the palm with a smile on his face. When the tree took a turn upward, he dropped into a straddle and crabwalked his torso rapidly up the crown, where he stood up again, clinging to a few of the giant fronds. He plucked the small fruit of the coconut, no bigger than a large marble, and tossed one down. It struck Hugh's chair and bounced into the sand near his feet. Hugh looked at the fruit, then strained his neck and gazed up at the tree, where the boy did his best to hide behind some palm fronds. Hugh pretended not to see him, and three or four seeds flew down until one landed with an audible *ponk* on Hugh's head, and he set aside his book, turned in his chair and said, "I was looking for you."

The boy shimmied halfway back down the tree, then dropped. He stood and sprinted toward Hugh, and then rolled in the sand. Sitting up, he said, "Your family enjoying Oppenheimer Beach?"

Hugh had noticed the night before that while the boy spoke with a West Indian lilt, his English had the pointed diction and syntax of an Oxford don. Hugh glanced from the boy to a building back in the palms at the far end of the beach. He was aware that Robert Oppenheimer had spent some of his last years in the 1950s here, and that oddity had in some way attracted him. He hadn't known the locals called it Oppenheimer Beach; he had thought the name was Little Hawksnest.

"He be my granfadder," said the boy, now speaking patois with a grin.

Hugh laughed and said, "Oh, dat so?"

"Yes," said the boy. "Dey call me de Oppie."

"Right," said Hugh. "As in J. Robert Oppenheimer."

"Dat be de mon," said the boy, taking from the pocket of his bathing suit a small plastic bag, and tossing it to Hugh. "Forty dolla."

Hugh sniffed inside, and Oppie handed him some rolling papers and a lighter. He rolled a joint, took a long hit, and after hesitating for a second handed it over. Oppie took a hit, and handed it back, and after exhaling, pointed back up the steep hillside in the distance and said, "Me mother she grow de plant up dere."

"Your mother the pot grower is Robert Oppenheimer's daughter?" Hugh said, taking another puff.

"That's right," said Oppie, dropping the island patois, and a hostile look crossed his face for a second. Then he stood and said, "I've got to go."

Hugh jumped up. "Don't go. I owe you some money. Plus, I'm enjoying talking to you."

Oppie smiled and said, "I live here. I'm just going out to visit the reef. We can talk when I get back."

Hugh nodded, and took a hit off the joint. Oppie ran into the sea and dove underwater. Hugh was able to follow his dark shadow, and he seemed to stay under for a couple of minutes. Then Hugh lost track of him, closed his eyes, and puffed now and then on the rest of the joint until it burned his fingers. He heard the boy drop down next to him and he said without opening his eyes, "I have one important question for you, Oppie. Do you think the life of one of those parrotfish I assume are out there on that reef is as important as the life of a human being?"

"Of course."

"Do you think you can talk me through this?" Hugh said, opening his eyes and lighting another joint. "I guess what I am saying is—what am I saying?—to recap, you think the life of a human being is equal in value to that of a parrotfish. I guess we can assume your grandfather, shall we call him J? That he didn't agree?"

"I don't know," Oppie said, taking the joint and inhaling deeply. "Sometimes I wish I had met him, so I could ask him a lot of questions, like that one. I mean he moved here to this beach for a reason, right? He wanted to get away from people who questioned his politics, but he could have gone to Saigon or Uttar Pradesh. But he came here, to live on a beach with just one other family, and no road to Cruz Bay. He came out of all the places in the world. And every day he sat right here in his khakis with his pipe and a white shirt and he had martinis and looked out at the reef, and once a day before dinner he gathered some local kids and they all put on their snorkels and masks and swam around it for an hour."

"So you think he was responding to the reef like I bet you do?"

Oppie shook his head. "I'd like to think so. I mean of course he was to some degree. But he was also grabbing some lobsters for dinner."

Hugh opened his eyes wide. "Grabbing? You mean J. grabbed them with his hands?"

Oppie sighed and handed back the joint. "They don't have claws like Atlantic lobsters, just two long antennae. But he didn't really even have to swim over the reef to get them in the 1950s. He could just climb over those rocks down there to Hawksnest Beach, walk out to his knees, and pluck them from the rocks. Lobsters were everywhere. Now I see maybe one a month, and I kayak them out to Henley Cay, where nobody goes much. But my grandfather liked to swim once a day over the reef, and I'm glad he did, as you have to admit it humanizes him, although it also makes what he did with the bomb more complex. It would have been easier in some ways if Grandpa was insane, but yes, he appreciated the reef. My grandmother, who was his cook, told my mother that he said it was the best thing about St. John. Maybe when he was my age he appreciated things the way I do, but maybe no one around him saw that as a good thing, or even acknowledged that he had that capacity for wonder. Your name is Hugh, for example. But what if your real name was Harvey? And if no one ever called you Harvey, and thought you were insane when you said, "My name is Harvey." Well, over time it would take a very strong person not to begin to forget all about their true name of Harvey, or feel their 'Harvey-identity.' What I am saying is, if no one acknowledges your wonder, you begin to doubt it is in you, and slowly it just disappears. Then you are just Hugh Copley the stoned and cynical freelance photojournalist."

Hugh took a long drag, held it in his lungs while shaking his head. "How long have you been selling this shit to tourists?"

Oppie sat in the sand. "You mean about being the grandson of J. Robert Oppenheimer?"

"Yes, that."

Oppie stood up and walked down to the water. He dove into a wave and swam out, then rode a wave back in. When he stood, he whipped his neck around, sending his Rasta hair flying. He walked down the beach, then turned and waved for Hugh to follow him. Hugh jogged down the beach and then walked along next to him. He followed him up over some rocks at the end of the beach toward the mustard-yellow concrete building. There were rusted iron bars over the windows. Oppie got a key from under a conch shell, opened the door, and the two went inside. The floor was cool tiles, dank. Oppie took him into a back room and positioned him. There was a green anole lizard doing pushups on the ceiling, flaring its throat into a red sack angrily.

"There," Oppie said.

"What?" said Hugh.

"That's the spot my white aunt hung herself. This was her childhood home. She left it to the children of the Virgin Islands in her will."

Hugh wanted to hit the boy. He felt sick, and left the damp, mausoleum-like building. Outside he walked quickly out of the palm tree shadows back to the beach and stood looking at the waves cresting the brown coral tips of the reef. He found he was weeping, and brushed away the tears with the back of his hand. Then he relit the joint with shaking hands and took a deep inhale.

Oppie was next to him looking up at his face. "When I feel like you look, I go swim over the reef."

"You always loved the reef?"

"When I was five I was swimming alone over it," Oppie said. "I entered the water right here. It was on Easter, and there was a fish fry on this beach. A fish fry is a big West Indian community party, and the government opened the house where my aunt hanged herself, and half the island was here, and there was a scratch band and dancing. We don't have many of them anymore. I never like crowds, and didn't even then, so I went for a swim. And while I was looking at a giant brain coral with two angelfish swimming around it, I had the feeling that I was part of that brain coral, that there was no 'I,' and I banged my head pretty hard. My other grandfather, Mr. Jacob, was whelking over there on the rocks, and he jumped into the water in his long pants and grabbed me."

Hugh suddenly felt weak after another hit, and squatted down.

"I stopped banging my head on the reef after that," Oppie said, laughing. "But the feeling that the reef and I are the same thing pretty much stayed."

Hugh nodded. "You still can feel that?"

"Yes," Oppie said. "Although sometimes I feel it slipping away. Last year I was sure it would always be with me, but this year I spend more and more time underwater looking at the reef. It's safe there for me, for the most part."

Hugh took a hit, and looked out at the darkness under the blue water. "How do you get that feeling?" he asked, and shook his head, and looked at the joint. "Well, without this stuff in my lungs."

"It isn't hard," Oppie said. "Everybody who swims over a reef feels it to some degree. You do. I know you do because you're talking to me about it." He reached down and picked up a piece of coral. "The difference, I guess, in part is what you do about the feeling after you get out of the water," he said. "For example, did you feel something the first time you saw your wife?"

"My wife?"

"The first time. You felt something."

Hugh nodded. "Of course."

Oppie nodded. "And what did you do next?" he asked.

"Next?" Hugh laughed. "Well, it was in Senegal. I didn't know who she was, but I went up to her and took her hand and kissed her palm."

"And then what did you do?" Oppie asked. "I know you did something because now she's your wife."

Hugh reached up and pulled a leaf from a palm frond. "I know what you're getting at," he said, exhaling smoke. "But my wife is a woman, and yes, I chased her and sat outside her hotel and begged her to be with me. It took a few years. But she's a woman. I mean you can't marry a—"

"Maybe you can," Oppie said. He touched Hugh's arm. "You're dry. Why are you here talking to me when you could be out there with her? That's how the feeling grew with your wife, right?"

"But she's human," Hugh said, glancing at the boy, and then adding, "And there are other drives there, you know?"

Oppie glanced back at the house behind them and, smiling, said, "I know about other drives."

"Right," said Hugh. "I guess you do." Hugh touched Oppie's arm. "So the world is doomed?" he asked. "Is there nothing we can do?"

"My mother is waiting for me," Oppie said.

"I want to know if you think we are doomed," Hugh said. "I mean, is there nothing we can do?"

"I don't think there is," Oppie said. "I used to think there was a chance when I was younger, but I was just hopeful, the way the young are before they meet a lot of adults." He folded his arms, and reflected briefly. "I used to take people I thought were nice on swims over this reef. I'd show them the obvious tourist things like the parrotfish . . . and then if I thought they were amazed enough, if they came up blowing water out of their snorkel and choking because they forgot to breathe, I'd show them cooler things like the trumpetfish, the goatfish, or the squirrelfish, and if I really liked them, I'd show them a school of squid. You can tell everything about a person by how they respond to looking into the black eye of squid, or how the squid respond to them. They communicate with each other by changing color, you know." Oppie thought for a moment. "But too many people came up and wanted to know if they were good to eat. One father even went to a shore, came back with a net, caught one, and stood up on the reef and tried to eat it. He said it was sushi and put it in his mouth and bit the squid's head off. I had serious doubts about that man from the beginning, but his daughter came up crying after I showed her a blue tang school, so I gave her father a tour. When they got in their jeep to go, she jumped out and ran back down and grabbed me by the arms and begged me to hide her. I should have done it, because she was going to be killed by him. Everything is against a girl like that living past the age of twelve. It takes hundreds of years to grow a few inches of reef, but every second person I took out tried to stand on the coral, and they broke off hundreds of years of growth. I can't tell you how much that upset me. And that father, he didn't see the beauty in his little girl wanting to stay here forever because she was so moved by the reef. He dragged her back to the car, and when I tried to tell him he was hurting her, he spit on me and called me a nigger. I think right when his spit hit me, like the spit was knowledge, I knew he would kill that little girl in a few months, or that maybe he had killed her right then, and also that the world was doomed. You know how my grandfather said "I have become death" when he saw his bomb explode in the Nevada desert? I realized right then that all of us, you and me too, we have all become death in the same way."

"I've been thinking about that, too."

"You know the bleaching on the reef? Whole sections just turn white as chalk. The living polyps die and they are just skeletons. No one is totally sure what causes it. That's what human beings are, a sort of white pox. Every human being alive right now, just by being alive, is a destroyer of life. You'd think people would just be sick with guilt, want to hang themselves or something."

"Do you?"

"I don't think so," Oppie said. "As long as this reef is still here, you'll find me here. I get up every morning at dawn to watch the sun rise over this bay, or I see a gecko crawling on a tree, or just termites running to rebuild their secret tunnels up and down a mahogany tree, and I just want to wake ten thousand times again to see everything there is in the world. But mostly I want to swim around this reef all day. Besides, there might be a giant plague or something that wipes out everyone, and gives the world some breathing space. But I doubt that will happen in time for this reef. If this reef died, I'd want to go with it; I wouldn't want to just look out here at the skeleton of a reef with no fish or octopuses or conch or polyps. There is one thing that might push me over the edge: if I see a single lionfish. The lionfish came in the ballast of tankers from Indonesia, and they take over, can eat their body weight in juvenile reef fish in a day. Once there is one, the reef is doomed. You kill one, and ten more are there in a month. They have dozens of awful poison spines. They are territorial and will attack you sometimes, or you might not see it and brush it. The last time I touched one by accident out on Lovango Cay, I had an allergic reaction to the toxins and had to be airlifted to St. Thomas. They said the next one would kill me. He turned and looked Hugh in the eye. "My mother is waiting for me up there. I have to water her plants and then go into town. I'll be back this evening, and maybe we can swim over the reef, you can look a squid in the eye, and I can see what they think of you."

"Just one more minute," Hugh said. "Don't you want to go to a university, get a PhD? You could change . . ."

Oppie drew in the air the shape of a mushroom cloud. "A lot of people I talk to on the beach tell me I should leave St. John and go to school stateside," he said. "I've talked to some of the better-educated people in the world on this beach." He shook his head. "But it is pretty clear education would be the death of me."

"The death of you?"

"Yes. But what I mean by 'me' is different than what you mean." Oppie laughed. "Anyway, education would kill my sense of surprise. It might make me too proud."

"Can you explain that?" Hugh said.

"Sure," said Oppie. "Most people I meet here are too proud. Not just about their education, or their money—that they can spend $3,000 for a week in a villa—but proud of their existence. Everyone thinks about themselves as if they made themselves. All the adults I meet on the beach are so proud, seem to imagine they mixed their own DNA the way I mix them a coconut and mango daiquiri." Oppie ran his fingers along his long black plaits of hair and then grabbed his chest with two hands, as if he was having a heart attack. "But I'm a surprise," he said. "My body is a surprise. Your body is a surprise. But I'm the only one who seems totally surprised to have a body. You may once have been, but you have forgotten to be surprised. But I think you might still remember. It would take first of all you *wanting* to be surprised—but I think if you go to bed and night and say, 'Please, make me more surprised,' it *might* happen." He suddenly reached out his bare foot and touched Hugh's foot with his own and said, "I have to go back to my mother." Hugh found himself standing, and almost bowing, before he caught himself and then yelled after the boy, "I want you to talk to my son sometime!"

That afternoon Hugh stood in the checkout aisle with one hand on a quart of eleven-dollar orange juice, his credit card flipping in the fingers of his other hand. The checkout girl took the juice out of his hand and ran the barcode, and did the same for his case of Red Stripe and a bottle of dark Cruzan rum. Then she touched his arm and pointed, and he awoke and asked for fifty dollars cash back, slid his card, signed, took the brown bag and the case in his arms and walked out of Starfish Market.

The lot was full of a hundred brand-new rental Jeeps, and the smell of fresh asphalt filled his nose in a sweetly putrid way. Hugh sat in his Jeep and smoked another joint while pressing the brake over and over with two bare feet, the wheeze of the hydraulic compression an alien pleasure in his toes. Eyeing the orange juice, he pulled out the bottle of rum. The winter trade winds nipped and scuttled whitecaps across the waters of the industrial harbor below, where dozens of trucks and Jeeps awaited the next barge to St. Thomas.

Hugh was surprised to hear his tires squeal when he pulled out. He drove rapidly up Centerline Road, sipping from a warm Red Stripe. The sun was losing its harsh noon rule, and moister and darker green tones played in the breezes on the steep hillsides; he smiled a few times as he took the switchbacks up Bordeaux Mountain. At the top he pulled over and gazed out over Coral Bay at the serpentine green arm of St. John's East End. It was an unreal vista, perhaps the most gorgeous he had seen in his years of travel around the globe, and Hugh wept so hard he was unaware he was violently punching the steering wheel, until a tourist tapped on his window and asked if he was OK, and he became aware of the pain in his knuckles, and that he had been blaring his horn with each punch.

He took North Shore Road and parked behind an old blue Land Rover. He got out and rested his hand on a plastic dinosaur that had been wired on as a hood ornament, and then scratched at the plastic with his fingernail. He skirted the locked iron gates that said OPPEN-HEIMER BEACH, wondering why he'd never noticed the sign before, and halfway down the ridged concrete driveway came upon a Rastafarian who was chipping at a coconut in his palm with a machete. Hugh said hello, and the man pointing with his machete said, "me Oppie in dat water."

He was swimming rapidly toward the boy when he saw him extending his arm toward a layered antler of staghorn coral. The boy's mask glittered, and he worried a barracuda might strike. He saw the hand suddenly flash back from the reef, and a fish darted out and seemed to attack the boy. The boy was grabbing it to his chest, or maybe he was trying to push it away, but the fight went for a few seconds, and then he was quiet, and gently swayed downward on his back to the shallow reef, on which he seemed to levitate.

THE BLACK BOX

Billy Weimar was called before an ad-hoc committee of several partners at Goldman Sachs. On the surface, it was to account for his
unexplained ten-day absence from work. But it had been more dra-
matic than that: When Goldman's in-house security came up empty,
the police had been called on the third day and a missing persons
report filed. In the search for Billy it was discovered that he hadn't
lived in his shabby studio apartment on West 125th for over two
years; his landlord said he just stopped paying his rent, left a room
full of thousands of dollars of computers and "hundreds of books
about black holes and the Big Bang and way-out-there shit like that,"
and disappeared. The landlord sold the computers, kept the depos-
it, and had no hard feelings about the "quiet little geeky guy" who
"never slept" and "lived like a monk." It was also curious that neither
Goldman's security nor the police could find any cybertrace of Billy.
It was known he had an iPhone, but if he did, there was no record
of him with AT&T or any other carrier. Nor was there any of Billy
on the web; his IP addresses drew blanks. Although it was known
he e-mailed in-house with work associates, his Goldman account,
when entered, displayed nothing but a photo of the iconic Rolling
Stones 'tongue' logo, with the tongue moving back and forth. His
fellow Quants on the seventh floor shrugged at all this, as if cyber-
invisibility was no great achievement. They expressed no particular
concern for Billy's welfare, but were clearly at a loss without him
working on the HFT (High-Frequency-Trading) or "Black Box" secret

program. Some wondered if he had taken the algorithmic recipe for HFT to another firm, or gone rogue with it. One of the few female Quants said without raising her eyes from a screen that she wouldn't be surprised if he had jumped off the George Washington Bridge. His mother, who lived in Larchmont, said he hadn't come for his last biweekly visit, and had no other information to offer, other than that "Billy was the opposite of his father," who, she informed them several times, had been until his death a well-known Ford Motor Company specialist on the floor of the New York Stock Exchange, a president of the American Libertarian Society, and a personal friend of Ayn Rand.

☞ ☜

Billy was sitting outside the meeting room with his hands on his knees when the double doors opened and he was ushered in. Those who had known him on sight were surprised by his dress, not that his dress was in any way surprising at first glance. He was wearing the corporate armor, a pinstriped suit with a striped rep tie. Several partners recognized it as a Harvard tie, which made sense, as Billy had gone there before heading on to MIT for a PhD in theoretical physics (a program he dropped out of just months before defending his dissertation). He wore on his left lapel the small American flag that had become in the last few years a necessary Masonic-like symbol of corporate conservatism. But though the whole assemblage was conventional, it was also off in a faintly theatrical way: the suit was a size or two too big, and the cuffs were rolled up once at the ankles, and the tie ended near Billy's navel. And the suit itself was striped in the wide chalk way that was more Al Capone than Timothy Geithner. In someone perhaps more socially and mentally normative, it would have been read as a clownish mockery of the Wall Street uniform, but as Billy Weimar was known as the Quant of Quants at Goldman, the eccentricity was overlooked today to a degree as a helpless geek's stab at normalcy, and all things considered even noted in the plus column, as Billy had been known to show up to work week after week in the same ratty Goldman Sachs T-shirt and dorky khaki pants without a belt, and his BO was infamous.

☞ ☜

When questioned about his disappearance, Billy was contrite, offering strangely simpering apologies, again very odd for Billy, who was known for his awkward abrasiveness. He said in his nasally voice that in recent months he had been working 24/7 on the Black Box project, and that he just had lost it and decided to drop out a little while, had "gone to the desert like Jesus when he was tempted by Satan with all the riches of the world," to "steal some R & R personal time' and "get his mojo back" so he could come back and take the "project over the finish line ASAP."

The phrasing was so false and odd, and so clearly said with mental quotes, that all the members of the committee sat silently for a few moments.

Then Billy spoke into the quiet, almost in a whisper, "The Black Box is almost ready."

It was as if Billy had said "a Midas machine that prints money by the billions is now on the seventh floor." The partners took deep breaths and smiled at each other and leaned back in their chairs and nodded benevolently at Billy. The partners had planned not only to rake Billy over the coals about his absence, but also, since it had been believed the Black Box project was floundering, they were prepared with a list of complaints about him compiled just for this meeting. His general disorder of person and workplace, his arrogant attitude when questioned, his seeming disdain for anyone at Goldman including his fellow Quants—how when John Burns, a senior vice president, had reached out and tapped him on the shoulder in the elevator to ask him to press the button, Billy had slapped his hand and yelled, 'Don't you ever touch me again' in such a hostile way that Burns was barely able to describe it. "He's a very angry man," said Burns in an e-mail to the committee. "I suspect he might be dangerous in a sort of Ted Kaczynski way, and I am not exaggerating. He scares me, and I think for the safety of all he should have a psychological evaluation imme-diately." Burns was not alone in saying, in so many words, that Billy gave off the scent of a sulfurous rage burning just below the surface of his bad skin. Several of those tapped for opinions on Billy said things like, "The guy could lose it and open up with a Glock someday in the cafeteria" or "Our Rain Man needs to be on meds and in anger management therapy," but one e-mail came in from a fellow Quant and said, "Goldman Sachs is shorting his phenomenal mental gifts. He is a deeply sad little man."

☞ ☜

But all worries about Billy in the committee room evaporated with the word that the Black Box project was a go. The word had been spreading among certain parties at Goldman Sachs that the project had met obstacles that, although not insurmountable, had thrown the project's timetable back many months, and many even questioned if it was plausible that one could ever "see the market's movement in advance" through the use of algorithms.

After a great deal of good cheer and very basic small talk by Billy about algorithms, he headed off, without taking a breath and in his nasal voice, into a soliloquy on how a black box full of these equations could be used to sniff out the direction of the market. It was all about bouncing packets of small orders in an infinitesimal fraction of a second off the market and cancelling them just as fast, in order to scrape off an actionable foreknowledge of the incoming huge buy orders of fund blockbusters like Fidelity or TIAA-CREF. Billy lost them all as he then headed into the mathematical minutiae, and finally one of the partners interrupted and asked when, *exactly*, he projected the Black Box might be operational?

Billy seemed not to hear.

The partner repeated the question, and everyone looked at Billy, who with half-closed eyes, gazing at a spot above and far beyond the heads of the committee, seemed to be in a sort of trance.

Ellen Furnal, a junior partner, stood and walked over to Billy and gently shook him by the arm and said, "Mr. Weimar, are you still with us?'

Without lowering his head or opening his eyes, Billy said in a whisper, "*For no one knows my little game, that Rumpelstiltskin is my name.*" And then Billy erupted in laughter. He found the Grimms' fairy tales hilarious and had memorized a dozen word for word. He liked and thought it right and just that at the end of the final 1857 version, Rumpelstiltskin "seizes his left foot and tears himself in two," as opposed to earlier versions in which he falls into an abyss, or simply runs off.

Before the committee could react to this oddness, Billy snapped open his eyes, sat up straight and said, "Excuse me, I haven't slept a lot in the last few days. You were asking about the Black Box? It should be ready to rock and roll within a week or so."

A few committee members shook their heads, as if to say, Have you ever seen such a weird little man, but then the good news about the Black Box washed over them again like a golden wave, and there were a few laughs, and when a senior partner stood and told Billy they didn't want to keep him any longer, and that all the committee asked was he try to smile a bit more around Goldman, the meeting was over.

☞ ☜

Billy ran back up to work up on the seventh floor. He spent a few minutes at his desk, and then ran back downstairs, leaping the final three steps to each landing. Ever since he was a boy in Larchmont, he had always jumped the final three steps. He wasn't sure why he did it, but had a deep sense of horror of the consequences of not following this ritual: something might steal from him his mathematical capacities, and thus leave him without any pleasures in this world. His two front teeth, now yellowed with hundreds of cups of Bewley's Tea, were fake from when he fell face-first onto a landing of his dormitory at Andover. But today Billy had the delicate sensation of flying, and a few times he jumped from the fourth and even, at the ground floor, the fifth step up, as if in celebration.

He was celebrating not his continued employment at Goldman—he knew the partners wouldn't fire him so long as the Black Box was coming along—but that he was going to attend a conference on theoretical physics at the Sheraton at Madison Square Garden, and in particular, listen to a talk by his best friend, the Norwegian physicist Viveka Karlsson, on CERN's search for the dark matter that held the universe together.

Viveka had been a few years ahead of Billy at MIT, and Billy had spent many late nights with her in discussions over string theory and black holes. As the years passed, those long discussions with Viveka seemed to Billy more and more clearly to have been the happiest days of his life. He had not, as he told the committee, been in "the desert," but had flown to Switzerland at the invitation of his old friend, and spent days by her side at the giant particle accelerator, looking over data. Billy had slowly realized while there that Viveka wanted to know more about how he, Billy, interpreted certain data that had run against the Standard Model of the Universe. In e-mails with Viveka over the last few months, Billy had seen samples of this data, and had provided an explanation so far-fetched that Viveka had simply sent back three letters in response: LOL. But then Viveka had bought him a ticket to Switzerland, put him up in an expensive hotel, and quizzed him, urged him to expand on how the slivers of data fit his napkin-doodled conjectures on why the invisible dark energy and dark matter that made up 96 percent of the universe was never diluted as the universe expanded. In a bar in Geneva, Billy drank ginger ale and expatiated to Viveka on a theory (one that left the "joke" of the idea of super-symmetric particles way behind) of why this invisible other "stuff"—which could only be detected by its nonlocalized gravitational effect—was always homogeneous in space and time, and spittle jumped off his lips in his excitement to convey the necessary geometric shapes of the strings he saw rattling in the fifth, sixth, and seventh dimensions. He added with a snickering and somewhat pleased afterthought that the LDC accelerator at CERN would never detect dark matter, because although it was composed of particles, they were particles that were not created in the first instant of the Big Bang, and thus were not "hot," but infinitesimally later, and were thus "warm," which the detector was not built to detect. In short, the twenty-mile oval of a multibillion-dollar machine would never be able to answer the question it had been asked about dark matter and dark energy; but Billy's cerebrum *could*.

And now Viveka was suddenly here in NYC to give a talk billed as revolutionary and shocking—although she had never told Billy about the talk and in fact had shut down communications since that night of ginger ale and dark matter and energy—and Billy (who had read about the talk on a CERN discussion board) ran up Fifth Avenue, after sitting on bench near Central Park lost in new visions of strings vibrating in the fifth and sixth dimensions until a change in the breeze and the dying light in the leaves awoke him to his lateness. He raced into the Sheraton, ran up the stairs (taking them like a musical scale, half whole half half whole, as was his ritual), and was stopped at the door to the conference by security. For some reason, they had his photo, and he was escorted out of the hotel. The guards told him as they left him that Viveka Karlsson had said he was stalking her, and asked him to be kept out or risk arrest.

It was impossible. Billy crossed Seventh Avenue and then stopped cold. He was still standing when the green light flashed and cars and taxis honked and veered and zoomed around him. He started to flap his arms, as he did when severely stressed, and looked like a small man-bird trying to take flight. He suddenly dashed back toward Madison Square Garden and into the Sheraton and up to the conference floor, where he spied around a corner at the guards. He walked across the hall and felt the knob of another door, and hoping it opened to the same conference room, he stepped inside and slid into a seat in the back.

☞ ☜

When the talk began Billy was still thinking about his interpretation of the dark-matter and energy data from CERN and how it exploded the conservative physicists' Standard Model of the "realistic" universe in favor of the mysteries of other dimensions and the delicious-to-ponder explosive possibilities of the fundamentally impossible. Then the first speaker came out, and it was not Viveka Karlsson, nor was it remotely a talk on dark matter or dark energy. It took a while for Billy to zero in on what this gray-haired man, tall and thin with an awful face, was saying, but he sat up straight when an old Polaroid of four Ecuadorian Indians flashed on the wall behind the dais. The Indians were no bigger than Billy, and naked except for a small cloth, with sticks in their noses, standing before the jungle, armed with spears more than twice their length. These were the Huaorani, and the minister railed on how four Christian missionaries had been killed back in 1956 when they tried to make contact. Billy's senses sparked.

The missionary said his own father was one of those killed, but how other missionaries had gone back again, despite the danger. Slowly the cannibal Indians, some of the most violent and murderous natives in Latin America, had been Christianized and civilized. The audience of two hundred broke into loud applause, and Billy found himself standing and cheering wildly in his braying voice. Hymns were sung, and looking at the photo of the four Indians that remained on the screen, Billy found himself opening up for the first time to strange, exhilarating, almost violent emotions.

The talk ended with an appeal to join their missionary work, and Billy suddenly felt like a man possessed by a stranger. For the minister was standing on stage pointing for those who were willing to join him on the stage right now, and Billy was pushing past the others in his row to get to the aisle, and people were patting him on the back and yelling things like "Praise the Lord" and "Amen, brother, you have heard the call!" When Billy looked down on the stage, it looked like the minister was pointing right at him, and it was like he was being pulled out of his life, this stranger within him was magnetized by some force up on that stage. As Billy descended the aisle, people turned to smile and cheer and clap for him, as if he was a hero. There were a few others around the auditorium also making their way forward. And as Billy walked he found that he was looking past the missionary, and it was as if the four Indians in the photo were the true force pulling him to the stage, calling to him from the edge of the jungle where they stood with what looked like spears but might have been blowguns, decorated in river-mud paint, and Billy was seized by a strange terror, and turned and tripped and ran up the aisle and out of the auditorium.

☞ ☜

That night, Billy took the bus from Penn Station out to Larchmont, and walked in his distinctly toe-bouncing geek-gait from the station to the huge old house at 11 Woodbine, where his mother Bippy (born Beatrice) still lived. He visited her every other Sunday. Once it was every Sunday, but Billy found the experience so mentally draining that for twenty-four hours afterward he would lose interest even in his algorithms back at Goldman. How hard he worked was Billy's chief, and perhaps only, virtue, to his mother.

When he walked up the brick pathway to the three-story twelve-bedroom house he hated—a mansion by any normal definition, except on this street in this town where all the houses were this large—he knew she would greet him from the top of the stairs, as he stood under the dusty chandelier, with the words, "My son William is here from the city to take me to lunch at the club." She would be dressed for tennis in a short white skirt, white Tretorn sneakers, and a tight white Lacoste shirt that displayed the size and firmness of her sixty-year-old breasts. She was a gin-and-tonic alcoholic and had slept with every available "powerful" Wall Street man in Larchmont, although to Billy she liked to pretend she was a virgin saint to the memory of Billy's father.

Bippy had lost most of the millions her husband left her to one stockbroker after another. All they had to do was call her at cocktail hour and flirt and she was ready for any churning in her account. She told her sister in La Jolla she had fucked in eleven rooms and lost $11 million, and there was one room and $1 million left, and no servants, which in part accounted for the petrified dog shit to be found all over on the third floor. She collected Pekingese dogs (in the flesh and in porcelain) because they were once owned by the emperor of China, and as Billy watched her come down the stairs, seven of the creatures—to Billy, ugly little mops with smashed faces—nipped and growled at his heels, and Billy kicked them gently and surreptitiously away.

Billy took out his Blackberry, which he used as a shield against his mother. She believed when he took it out he was checking the market, and when he typed she was sure he was placing market-making trades of a "brutal" nature. His father had loved words like "brutal" and said a "killing" of a trade was where everyone on the NYSE floor could hear his balls clang together like the closing bell.

Of the many things that stood between mother and son, the most obvious was that Bippy had never asked Billy to take over her dwindling trust fund; she thought him, as he once heard her say to Ann Cabish at the club when he was in eleventh grade, "a bit of a fluff, and an embarrassment to his father." He was able to hear her rattle on about her disappointments with her only child because Billy in those years, to escape the torments of his peers, would crawl under the slatted cedar deck of the club and sit until cocktail hour was over and Bippy would drive the Mercedes drunkenly back to Woodbine asking Billy if her shoulders looked burned.

One day Billy sat by accident directly beneath his mother at her "official" table near the pool. "We don't know where he came from," said Bippy in a loud confidential whisper to her friend Margaret Earle. "My brothers are all big, aggressive alpha males, Billy's father was almost a cannibal he was so virile, but somehow we ended up in the baby lottery with this changeling. His father is sure he'll be eaten alive if he ever tries to work on the Street. Frankly, if I knew the goods we were being sold, I would have had an abortion."

As Billy mused on the word *cannibal* while staring intently at his Blackberry and his mother took the final step of the palace stairs, two things happened. It started to rain, slashing on the leaden windows with the random stained-glass coat of arms, and a basso profundo voice called from the hallway, "Bippy? Bippy?"

It was one of his mother's "friends," a brick-faced, nose-veined, shiny-bald managing partner at Morgan Stanley. The club date with his mother was off due to rain and Charles Holsten. Which was good for all, as in truth they never made it to the club when Billy came to visit. Something always happened to keep Bippy from having to enter the sacred grounds with her weaselly son where her alpha-husband once strode. As Bippy embraced Charles, Billy headed off to the kitchen, then scooted down the maid's stairs to the basement.

In the distance he could hear Charles Holsten's voice as if in competition to fill the whole house, and Bippy's laugh, which sawed through the floor. Billy stood in the dark with his arms wrapped around his sunken chest and hyperventilated, until finally he felt his heart slow. He stood in the musty darkness, as he had for hundreds of hours as a boy escaping the eye of his father, an eye so iron-pike-like in its severity that Billy always had the sense he might stab his son, break off a leg, and gnaw on it like a hambone, all the while discussing the day's market moves in the parlor.

Billy slowly reached out in the darkness until his fingers felt the rough wood of an old wine crate, and for the next four hours, hands in his lap, he sat on it, safe and content. He was the same way at Goldman; he spent many hours alone thinking in the men's room. The motion-detector lights went off after thirty seconds of stillness, and sometimes Billy sat so long on the toilet seat his legs went numb: he imagined himself just a Maglite of consciousness, a small spark of wonder, considering from a nearly empty corporate headquarters in Manhattan the hypothesis of dark matter, the mysterious stuffing that might hold everything together.

☞ ☜

Several partners—especially those who knew the basics of what Billy Weimar and those working with him were up to—were apt to downplay his oddities as the eccentricities of a genius-level Quant, and a few liked to toss around the movie A Beautiful Mind and suggest that as long as he builds the Black Box for Goldman, who cares if later on he falls, like schizophrenic John Nash, into a series of imaginary relationships with Chinese spies and ends up tied down in a psychiatric hospital?

The seventh floor was called by a few The Ant Farm, as if the Quants were insects busily working while being watched safely from behind glass by actual humans, who marveled at their strange, incomprehensible, obsessively algorithmic industry. Those partners who had tried over the years to talk to Billy Weimar always found the talk circling back to CERN and the particle accelerator and the search for the origins of the universe. Weimar's friends at MIT were mostly now working in Geneva, and when his mind wasn't on the Black Box it was on gluons and nuons. When he spoke about CERN his face lost its sneer and took on almost a holy glow, along with a deep and pained look of loss. Over time, others tried to talk about CERN with him, but he refused to engage with them. Sometimes people looking over his shoulder reported seeing physics websites open on his desktop.

It was understood by the few who cared to unravel the heart of Billy Weimar that the great regret of his life was not to be involved in theoretical physics. He had left physics impetuously, said one partner who knew Billy's father, right after Billy's father's sudden death. Billy's father had hated him, the story went, for choosing pure science over using his mathematical gifts on the street, and the day after the old man crumpled to the floor of the NYSE, Billy dropped out of MIT's physics program and went to Vegas to count cards. He worked alone, moved from casino to casino, never won too much, and used his comped rooms as a sanctuary to consider the fundamental questions of theoretical physics without the restrictions of academia.

When the casinos finally sniffed out that he was beating the house up and down the Strip, he was banned, but the Mirage vice president who exposed him said he would put Billy up in a suite if he would work on a program to facilitate fair trading on something called the Hollywood Stock Exchange. This led Billy to a contract to make impossible illegal front-running, or Black-Box trading, in the "Dark Pools" of hundreds of millions of dollars of trading happening off the actual floor of the New York Stock Exchange. What Billy's father used to do as a "specialist"—matching up buyer and seller on the floor of the Stock Exchange—was now done by computer. Billy sold most of the rights to the program that would banish front-running to Cantor Fitzgerald, who sold it to Goldman Sachs. The paperwork regarding the sale was lost in the Twin Towers on 9/11. Goldman took the software that was meant to *stop* front-running and asked Billy to tweak it into a black box designed to strip millions a day from an unsuspecting market.

☞ ☜

After three straight nights of chocolate bars and testing algorithms, Billy wandered the trading floor at Goldman as if he was Moses come down from the mountain with the Ten Commandments (except they were inscribed in code not stone), and he looked out of his good eye at the traders with the same look Moses wore when he saw the Sodomites worshipping the golden calf. He stood there, hands on hips, little chin elevated, and slid a hand in his tight shirt and pinched his right nipple; twisted it erect as he considered with evident disdain the red- and yellow-tied proles before him feverish with fear and greed as they in so many ways humbled themselves before the market god. He struggled to adjust his chin higher, to project the might of his certainty that he was a superior being now; that the coming perfection of his algorithms was elevating him beyond them.

In the hand not pinching his nipple he carried a yellow folder brimming over with equations, the symphonic scribblings of his sleepless nights in his tiny office, and as he found he could not lift his chin any higher, he slowly raised the folder over his head and waved it like a semaphore signaling nothing but: I, William Weimar, Quant, am better than all of you greedy, hustling fucks.

A few traders glanced over at little Billy fanning the air, and then Carl Holman stood from his desk, circled behind Billy, and cuffed him with cupped hands over both his ears. He did it just as Billy's arm was on an upswing, and the algorithms flew into the air. Deaf, Billy dropped to his knees and crawled around, clutching his papers to his chest madly and crying out in a strange guttural language.

Ben Phelps, the trader closest to Billy at the time, and who had grown up the child of charismatic Christians in Pasadena, told some colleagues at Royce's later over shots that he was sure Billy was "speaking in tongues" and that it was probably Aramaic, in any case some old biblical language, but that it sure as fuck wasn't "Wall Street English." Standish Clemson, who had been forced to listen to Harry Potter on the way to Stratton Mountain from Darien last weekend with his three kids in the back of his Cadillac SUV, said it was Parseltongue, the language of the Slytherins, and of snakes.

This last view took hold as the dominant meme, for a couple of reasons: First, Billy wore black round thick glasses like Harry Potter. Second, he also had a significant scar like Potter. Not on his forehead, but on his nose, from when a group of boys had silently jumped him on the way home from junior high, and Curt Stephens (who later died in Afghanistan) had smashed his face against a telephone pole so badly the nasal bone had to be rebuilt.

☞ ☜

Things went steadily to shit at Goldman. There was something Tourette's-like about his spastic need to let other Masters of the Universe, from partners, to traders, to economists, know how he disdained their calculating, their guesswork, their market manipulation, their hedging and spreads and percentages, puts and shorts and calls; he had to let them all know in his stuttering nasal voice that he, Weimar, had no time for plays or forecasting or sales or politics or deception or thievery; for he was the one who owned the market's mind; to him and his black box filled with perfect algorithms she had at last submitted. He knew what the market wanted before she knew; he had jumped on Einstein's back and pierced the space-time continuum with his algorithms to send golden trades back from the future to the foolish, desperate mortals screaming on the trading floor.

One morning he snorted in an equine way at a managing partner by the name of Ramos Costalani, who had just nailed $10 million on a play on Serbian dinars against the French franc. There had long been jokes about what to do with the Quants, but it was a gray area: So many at Goldman were number geeks, arithmetic eunuchs, that it was hard to say someone was over the line, off the reservation, hard to identify the boundary between an overdose of Quanty-Asperger's, and an obnoxious and grandiose in-your-face Rain Man. But for years it had been building, the distant communal sense that Weimar specifically was a Quant gone feral, and that something had to be done. There were fantasies of tossing him late one night out a trading floor window; or sending an overweight hooker with the murderous gifts of La Femme Nikita to sit on his face and smother his geekhood into a righteous submission. There was an e-mail thread: "Ways to Whack Billy Weimar." Someone sent around a crude drawing of Weimar with head and feet in a magician's black box, and a man who looked like the CFO of Goldman raising a saw as if to cut him in two.

And then Billy Weimar flipped the on switch of his magic Black Box, and a Niagara of money unheard of in the history of the Street was released: For one hundred days in a row Goldman Sachs made $100 million a day. Weimar's Cray Supercomputer of a brain had invented a machine that was the Holy Grail of greed: a way to look at the other guy's poker hand and even pluck away his aces. Every partner, every employee at Goldman owed it all to Weimar: bonuses that year from

$100 million down to fifty thousand for some secretaries were courtesy of the metro geek with the laugh like a mule and the lazy right eye that drifted when he calculated.

And maybe it was that: the idea that this midget of a man with the pubic-hair attempt at a Van Dyke beard was flaunting his superiority; that this boy-geek with the encephalitic head had bigger cojones than all of them in terms of being a different sort of Rain Man; it couldn't help but produce testicular contortion in the elephantine egos of the Goldmanites. His Black Box took their white-collar financial leger-demain and made it Lilliputian; for little Billy Weimar had made the Delphic bitch-goddess of the market kiss his scrawny ass.

At the end of the golden run of $100 million days it became clear that others now understood the recipe to Billy Weimar's secret algo-rithmic sauce. And everyone from partner down who ever talked to Billy for five minutes at the Ant Farm wanted to take credit for the Golden Shower (for that's what it was called by some), and Billy's pres-ence around Goldman made it hard to rewrite history and grab credit. So talks were held, and when it was clear Billy had shot his wad, the word came down to send him packing. It wasn't hard to do: Billy's right to a percentage on the software had gone down in the rubble of the Twin Towers, and he had signed a joke of a contract with Goldman when he came on board. He was oblivious about these things anyway.

And so his keys were taken away, his photos of CERN stripped from his workspace, and he was told not to come back on Monday. Goldma-nites loved this firing, it was too perfect: the guy who conjured billions for the firm with his big head and his Black Box was kicked in the ass into the street. It was cannibalistic and almost immediately mythic: "You hear what they did to little fucking Weimar? They. Kicked. His. Ass. Out." It was made that much better by how Weimar had taken the news: he groveled and begged and refused to go and said crazy shit like Goldman was his life, until security had to carry him bodily from his office and place him a few blocks from the doors near the Thirty-Seventh Street subway. That a security guard had to give him fare for the train, and that after he gave the little fuck money, Weimar said, "Where should I go?"

The guard said, "Go home, Weimar."

Weimar looked so blank the guard said, "Are you telling me you don't have an apartment in New York City?"

Billy Weimar said, "I lived at Goldman. I was there all the time anyway."

The guard said, "Man, you got a credit card, and you must have millions in the bank, right?"

Billy nodded.

The guard said, "Then you got the world by the balls. Be glad you got away from those fucking jackals. When they whistle for the Four Horsemen of the Apocalypse just to sweep up the last five bucks, you'll be long gone. What they are is evil, Billy. I am telling you to run, run away, as fast and far in this world as you can go to save what little bit you got left of your immortal soul."

Billy was suddenly listening.

And the guard said, "You get on a plane tonight, go anywhere in the world, stay in the best hotels, and live like a little fucking Midas for the rest of your born days."

☞ ☜

The plane left Newark for Quito at 6:00 p.m. after sitting on the runway for an hour with the air-conditioning off. He was still wearing the blue Goldman T-shirt he had worn the day he was fired. There was a womblike, cosseting warmth to the 747, and while others sat sweating, complaining on cell phones in Spanish and drinking, Billy pushed up the center armrest, curled into the fetal position, and had a nice sleep for the first time in days.

When he awoke, he was at thirty-five thousand feet. A NASCAR race was on the TV ahead of him. Billy was awash with a pain that threatened to pull him down to earth, for the cars whipping the oval reminded him of the LHC particle accelerator at CERN, and his former friend Viveka Karlsson. He thought of his childhood home on Woodbine Street in Larchmont, and how at age ten he had taken apart the family's old cathode ray TV in the basement, when he became curious about how particles moved in a vacuum. For Billy it hadn't been far from that basement TV dissection to his theories on dark matter to Viveka in Geneva, but somehow Billy felt he had taken a wrong turn, and now it was all just darkness.

After a few ginger ales, Billy unbuckled and made his way back to the bathroom. He saw the man in the last row of the plane, and the two locked eyes. Billy stopped before him and the older man said, "You heard the call."

Billy shook his head.

The missionary took his hand in his cold grasp and said, "They called to you, didn't they?"

At that moment the sunset entered the cabin and bathed Billy in golden light.

"Who?" Billy said, though he knew exactly. The Indians had called to him; he was on the plane because he hadn't been able to banish the image of those four Indians with spears. He stumbled into the bathroom, but when he came out and tried to pass, the missionary reached out and pulled him into the seat next to him.

Neither spoke another word until they landed in Quito, but once an hour the missionary reached out and patted him on the head and repeated, "They called to you."

Billy and the missionary traveled together on a bus from the capital to the city of Puerto Francisco de Orellana, and from there by taxi to the River Napo, a tributary of the Amazon. There they boarded a "Rumba Nautica," a motorized barge with the body of a jet humorously welded above the waterline as the cabin. Billy looked out at a blank riverscape punctured miles beyond with the red flares of natural gas.

When they docked at Pompeya, the minister asked his name and wrote it on some official government paperwork, and they were waved through the oil company's security checkpoint. A soldier stretched and yawned, raising his submachine gun above his head. For the next two hours the missionary and Billy sat in the back of a flatbed truck on a gravel road, and as the road crossed the Rio Tiputini, the missionary pointed out the settlements of the Huaorani people. Billy understood this was the name of the Indians he had seen in the photo, but here they were wearing Western clothes, and working with machetes.

When Billy asked, the missionary said, "These Huaorani have already been saved."

The truck stopped by a narrow, muddy river, with the forest close on either side, and the two set off in a small boat. The minister leaned close to Billy and murmured, "Tell those in your heart that called to you that you are almost there, with the good news of their salvation."

Billy saw a sign for RESERVA COMUNITARIA KICHWA, and the missionary said, "We are in Yasuni National Park now." The river bent like a serpent, and Billy saw giant trees that arose from the forest. He spotted a turtle on a log that turned its head to look at him with its ancient eyes, and right then red howler monkeys shrieked from the forest, and Billy jumped like he was shocked, and the missionary laughed and slapped his knee.

The driver of the boat pointed out an anaconda back in the foliage, and as he spun around to give them a better view, explained that the Huaorani believed when you died you were on a trail in the jungle and came face to face with a giant boa. Jump it, or return as a termite. The missionary frowned. Soon they docked at the mission and stepped ashore. Right away it was clear to Billy that something was wrong. The mission, a complex of a dozen thatched houses around a church and school and a few other corrugated metal buildings, was silent and seemingly empty, and the missionary who had told Billy that he was always greeted with great affection by his "children" looked shocked and angry.

Billy was told to follow the missionary, who strode across the dirt of the compound calling in Huaorani to his children. Then he said something like, "We shall see what Babae Ima has to say," and yanked Billy along a jungle trail. In an hour, Billy was seated in the long hut of clan leader Babae Ima, who seemed no friend of the missionary, and who shook open a bag until a skull covered in silken black hair rolled across the floor to stop against Billy's shoes. The minister closed his eyes and mumbled a prayer while Billy reached out and lifted up skull by the temples as if holding the head of a friend, and had the strange feeling that he was meant to be here.

The minister jumped up and yelled at Billy, who placed the skull back in the bag held open by Babae Ima.

On the way back to the mission village the two heard a helicopter, and soon after met Inspector Juan Suarez, who told the missionary, who told Billy, that a few days earlier a group of Huaorani men, led by Babae Ima and armed with rifles, had gone three days deep into the million-acre "Intangible Zone," a preserve of the fierce Tagaeri, one of the world's most reclusive tribes, and slaughtered several dozen Tagaeri, including women and children. Suarez had already interviewed Babae Ima once, and said Ima claimed it was in retaliation for the Tagaeri killing their tribal member Carlos Omene ten years earlier. And since the Huaorani have no sense of past and present, the killing was arguably reasonable. But Suarez said Babae Ima was paid in Spanish lumber by Columbian loggers for the killing of the Tagaeri, and that the loggers had been paid by oil companies who wanted to drill under the Intangible Zone and needed the last hundred Tagaeri, known by the Ecuadorian government as the "People Who Lived in Voluntary Exile," sent down the river of history.

Billy was giddy on the helicopter ride up the Tiguino River. He loved the sound of "The People Who Lived in Voluntary Exile" in the "Intangible Zone." Suarez had invited the missionary and Billy (thinking him a junior clergyman) as he flew alongside two other large military helicopters filled with thirty soldiers to the site of the massacre. Suarez wanted the missionary along as he was an expert in speaking Huaorani and had an encyclopedic knowledge of these tribes and of what had befallen them since they had met their first *cohuori*, or outsiders, in the 1960s, when they were still shooting peccaries from canopy trees with curare-tipped arrows. This was Suarez's first visit to the site of the massacre. He said he had a respect for the fierceness of the Tagaeri, who had marched into isolation in 1950 led by a warrior Taro; they were, said Suarez, the last "free people on planet earth," so he had, out of a combination of sympathy and caution, taken his time to gather information and soldiers before flying in.

For a few minutes they flew without speaking, and Billy craned his head in all directions and saw nothing but jungle. Suarez yelled over to him that "the Indians here believe the entire world was once forest," and that "only in the forest were they safe from the witchcraft of cohuori," and with that he pointed to himself and Billy.

The helicopters circled around an opening in the canopy as everyone craned to look for living Tagaeri. Only corpses were visible, strewn around the dirt and grass of the jungle floor. A communal hut had been burned. The helicopters landed, and the soldiers raced into position and quickly began to dig shallow trenches in which they lay with their rifles pointed toward the tangled forest. The dead lay all about, and they were almost all women and children. There was one old man decapitated in a hammock.

"If the oil companies murder the women and children," said Suarez to Billy, who marched by his side as he examined and photographed each corpse, "they know there will soon be no more Tagaeri. It's biology."

Inspector Suarez took time with the decapitated old man. As well as headless, the man had been left gored by a Waorani spear. Suarez pulled it out and said it probably belonged to Babae Ima, and was left as evidence that this was a clan-on-clan killing, and thus subject to tribal law, which meant in the end nothing could be done by the Ecuadorian government.

He handed the serrated fifteen-foot spear to Billy and said, "How would you like to be hunted by one of these terrible things?"

According to the report of Inspector Suarez, Billy said something like, "I won't die a termite," and then for the next half hour walked around with the spear in his hand. When Suarez yelled for everyone to get back on the helicopters, Billy stood still as a primitive idol, the weapon upright in his hand. The helicopters powered up, the dust flew around the clearing, and Billy for a second was lost to sight as everyone clambered aboard.

It was at the moment the dust cleared that Billy turned, dropped the spear, and walked across the trampled grass and into the jungle. Inspector Suarez jumped out of the helicopter and ran across to where he had disappeared as the helicopters powered down and the soldiers poured out.

HOTEL PALESTINE

A few days after the fall of Baghdad in April 2003, Ann Prendergast left the hospital after a miscarriage and slipped over the border from Amman, Jordan (after spending the night alone in an empty border station when her Iraqi driver left her there in a dispute over sex), and after a tough and often terrifying journey across the western Iraqi desert ended up at the Hotel Palestine in the bed of a journalist who days earlier had been killed by U.S. troops. The city was on fire, almost post-apocalyptic, as looters continued their sweep. For two days she sat in her room and replayed her last night with her senior-attaché husband, Alexander, in the bedroom of their apartment in Amman. That night he had rubbed her belly with rose oil and told her nothing he had believed about America was true, and that he wanted to resign from the State Department and for them immediately to emigrate to Iceland in time for their daughter's birth, so that they might both be reborn into innocence with their baby. That night he also took a midnight bath with a stack of memoranda, a bottle of single-malt scotch given him by Donald Rumsfeld, several dozen Xanax, a bootleg tape he made of the Grateful Dead in Philadelphia in 1981, and in the morning she found him, the only lover she had ever known, his angry blue face in a plastic bag almost hidden by floating papers.

On her second night in Baghdad, Ann finally left her room and climbed to the roof of the hotel. She found it a circus of journalists and tented media equipment, as well as a steady stream of talking heads:

former political exiles, tribal sheiks, ex-Iraqi army officers. There were nightly battles between U.S. troops and Iraqi resistance fighters. When the sun went down, the white phosphorus flares went up, anonymous machine guns pocked in the dark, and explosions drummed off distant buildings. For the next week, Ann stood at the edge of the hotel roof every night in khaki cargo pants and a long-sleeve T-shirt and observed the war as if it was on CNN. She had the terrifying sense that she wasn't even there, at the Hotel Palestine, and that it was some stranger hidden within her, some previously unknown Ann Prendergast, who had torn out the IV, run out of the Navy hospital, emptied her bank account, and hired a driver to take her to Baghdad.

One night there was a sudden silence all over the city. And then the power went out in the Hotel Palestine, and before the generator kicked in, a shadow placed in her hand a plastic cup filled with vodka. She turned and drank it down as she looked over the dark city. Surprisingly gentle lips kissed the top of her spine. When the lights came back on the roof, and machine-gun fire crackled the silence, she turned and looked down at the empty red cup. She held it up and sniffed the vodka, gazed at the reporters. No one looked at her. The next morning, Ann awoke at dawn and grabbed a satellite phone she found left in the lobby, as well as some MREs, and that night, she invited the monk-balding Angus Smith, a cameraman who happened to be from her hometown of Charlotte, North Carolina, to her room. He promised if he could just hold her every night, he'd get her a freelance contract with CBS News Radio. Few asked any questions right away about her nonexistent journalistic background, and when one did, she replied in her best wife-of-a-senior-diplomat-southern-girl voice, "Hong Kong . . . Calcutta, Kabul, why do you ask?" These were all places she had lived with Alexander over fifteen years.

Two days later Ann had a contract from CBS, and as she climbed the stairs to the roof of the Hotel Palestine, she passed a small and thin Iraqi woman in a long light-blue dress carrying a baby who could not have been more than six months old. A baby girl: widely spaced urgent brown eyes, a crop of soft black curls, dimpled arms wrapped tightly around her mother's neck. Ann smiled and waited as they passed and then followed them, mesmerized as the baby processed the chaos around her on the roof while the woman asked one journalist after another if anyone needed an interpreter. They looked at her like she was insane when she said with finality that as there was no one else in this world to care for her baby, wherever she went to report, her baby would come with her.

When it looked like the Iraqi mother was heading back down the stairs after finding no takers for her services, Ann ran over to ask if she could help. "I hope so," the mother replied with a tired smile. She told Ann in rapid, broken English that her name was Leyla, that her baby's name was Haddiyah, which means "gift" in Arabic, that she had been a teacher and a translator before the war, and that she wanted to work with a foreign journalist. She also said that her husband, Malik, a "very good-looking" pharmacist, had suffered a nervous breakdown during the "Shock and Awe" bombing campaign and that she now needed to be both breadwinner and caregiver for her husband and daughter. Her Shiite family had disowned her when she married Malik, as he was Sunni, so she was alone in Baghdad. Leyla said that she had no choice but to bring Haddiyah everywhere she went, and that with the help of the neighbors, her husband was strapped with ropes to his bed when she left the apartment, so that "he would not hurt himself or a stranger."

Ann knew she needed someone she could trust to be her ears and voice if she was going to be a reporter. And Leyla was clearly not only well educated (she talked as if she was the last defender of Langston Hughes, Edna St. Vincent Millay, James Baldwin, and Paul Robeson), but it turned out she had stellar credentials: She had worked as an interpreter for the British Council in Jordan before the war. She was also direct: she said she hated her own people for their religious madness, hated her own parents for their obsession with money, and deeply believed nothing but good would come from the Americans in Iraq. And she clearly had the guts to continue working, even with an infant, in one of the most dangerous places in the world. Ann hired her on the spot. Leyla had been making fifty dollars a month before the war; Ann offered her five hundred. They joked that they were the only wartime news team in history with a baby.

Leyla became Ann's lifeline as a reporter. Every morning they met in the lobby, and Ann would scoop plump (her mother said she used to be fatter before the war) Haddiyah into her arms and cuddle her on her lap as Leyla opened her notebooks and told the gossip from the Iraqi street. Ann had never met anyone as unapologetically curious as Leyla, who wondered about the inflow of Iranian cigarettes as a signal of the growing influence of Iran with the Shiite insurgents, or how the decreasing artistry and increasing crudity in graffiti was a sign of the validity of rumors of coming suicide bombings against the Americans. She also scoured the Arabic-language newspapers and broadcasts and chased down tips from women on the street both Shiite and Sunni, from beggars and prostitutes to former professors or wives of the endlessly morphing political and business establishment. She knew no fear of talking to men, either: With Haddiyah in her arms she spoke to politicians and policemen, insurgents and even infidels, such as American soldiers. Some of her best tips came from children, especially girls stuck in their apartments twenty-four hours a day, week after week, who kept a cat's eye on the street around the edge of heavy curtains.

The two set out daily with baby Haddiyah, a notepad, and a tape recorder to do "man on the street" interviews. Iraqis had begun swarming Firdos Square to complain about the lack of basic necessities and law and order. At first people were thrilled to see the baby, and were only too happy to share their hopes. Within a short time, though, the Iraqi street became increasingly anti-American and more dangerous; people felt the U.S. wasn't doing anything to help them, and that the troops were being too heavy-handed in their tactics. Marines set up checkpoints around the hotel zone of Baghdad. The three reported daily, and once Ann got a handle on the techniques of putting together a radio report, her editors at CBS professed to be very pleased with the stories she and Leyla were filing.

By spring 2004, the situation reached a crisis point. U.S. troops were fighting Shiite militias in the south and Sunni insurgents in the west. American casualties soared, and Iraq's infrastructure disintegrated. It was more dangerous for Ann to even leave the hotel, never mind march around the city with an Iraqi woman and a baby. But Leyla never faltered or mentioned risk, and the two were assigned stories of larger import, such as covering major developments involving both the U.S.-led coalition administration and the various Iraqi leaders vying for power. Angus still asked for nothing more than holding Ann every night, but he moved out of the Hotel Palestine when he took a job with the new U.S.-funded Iraqi TV station so he could live closer to the Convention Center, and he slept over less and less frequently. On May 1, President Bush declared the end of combat operations, and the marines were pulled out of Baghdad, leaving chaos.

And then one morning Leyla whispered to Ann in the red leather chairs of the lobby a scoop no journalist on the roof had any inkling of: villagers in Al Hillah, a Shiite town near the ruins of ancient Babylon, sixty miles south of Baghdad, were uncovering mass graves containing the remains of thousands massacred by Saddam's Sunni-dominated regime after a failed uprising in 1991. Ann jumped in a car with Leyla and Haddiyah, and they were the first reporters on the scene. For a while they were lost in farmland; then they came upon streams of Iraqis walking down a narrow dirt road, and then to a field behind a farm with hundreds of people gathered around several large Mitsubishi excavators. Ann and Leyla got out of the car and walked closer, and there was wailing and yelling all around them. The jaws of the excavator opened and deposited a load of dirt, and Ann saw several human bones, a crutch, and a prosthetic leg. Onlookers pawed through the piles looking for something they recognized of their brothers, fathers, sisters, mothers, children. ID cards were discovered, waved, and names called out.

Ann interviewed the farmer who owned this field. He explained that after the Shiite uprising here against Saddam in 1991, he saw truck after truck passing his farmhouse filled with people, then returning empty. He sliced his neck and covered his eyes and said to say anything would have meant death in the same pits. Over four days, thousands of Iraqis were taken to these pits and shot in the head. Ann uploaded her reports to CBS Radio from the killing field, and at the end of the day, after walking back to the SUV with Leyla, came upon an old woman in a hijab sitting on her bumper smoking a cigarette. Next to her was a clear plastic bag filled with bones. She shook a hand at Ann and started wailing. Leyla sat next to her talking soothingly as she cried out. It took half an hour to calm her, and then Ann did an interview with her in which she said her son had been one of the leaders of the uprising against Saddam, and it had only happened because America had told her son and others they would support it with helicopters and weapons.

On the way back to Baghdad, Leyla was quiet. Finally, Ann asked if she wanted to talk about it. Leyla said no, and somehow Ann started to confide how she now saw Leyla and Haddiyah as her family, and then told her about Alexander's suicide over his complicity in all the lies that led up to the war and then her own miscarriage. Leyla had one hand around a sleeping Haddiyah, and with the other touched Ann's cheek. Her hand was cool, and Ann kissed it. They drove in silence, and then Leyla said, "I want you to take my baby with you when you leave, and raise her in America, not in this country." Ann was shocked and said she would work to get them both out when the time came, but Leyla shook her head and insisted that she would never escape Baghdad. Before she knew what she was saying, Ann vowed that if something happened to Leyla, she would make sure her baby grew up in America with her.

"Thank you," said Leyla, taking her hand. "I am your sister now."

When they got back to the Hotel Palestine that night they found CBS was throwing a big party with music, food, and wine up on the roof. And then Ann learned that CBS had not run any of her reports on the killing fields at Al Hillah. Her editor told her the network was too busy with other news that day to cover a massacre from 1991.

That night, Ann considered leaving Baghdad. Most reporters stayed four weeks at a time, and she had been here three months. But by morning she realized she could not walk out on Leyla and Haddiyah.

☞ ☜

Baghdad soon became even more dangerous. The new police chief resigned in protest at U.S. military procedures. The streets were piled with rubbish, women and children were holed up at home, and a growing number of unemployed men entertained themselves with guns.

On Memorial Day, Iraqi insurgents killed the first U.S. soldier in Baghdad. From then on Ann taped to her hotel wall a list of every soldier killed in action; she documented where, when, and how each died. Several reporters who stopped by her room and saw the list commented that Ann "wasn't going to make it if she got so emotionally involved" and warned it was just going to get worse. But Ann continued her meticulous catalogue of the soldiers killed until the end of the year, when the number just got too high. There were new protests by former Sunni Baath Party police and army officers unable to find work and furious demonstrations by Shiite hard-liners who expected the U.S. to do more for them politically and economically. The only escape from the violence and mounting death: her daily time with Leyla and Haddiyah. She would run downstairs to see them every morning and let Haddiyah play with her microphone while Leyla gave her the gossip from the street. Ann took every chance she could to buy from the reopened shops nearby; a few sold baby clothes, and Ann loved surprising Leyla with new summer dresses and jumpsuits for Haddiyah.

Then Ann got sick just after covering a protest by Iraqi policemen at Assassin's Gate. It might have been from some chicken Leyla bought her on the street. She had dizzy spells, high fevers, and severe chills. It took a few spoiled blood samples and faulty test results before she was diagnosed with typhoid. Leyla bought medicine on the black market, and each day Ann took a vial of antibiotic fluids to a private Catholic hospital, where the nurses laughed at her when she rolled up her sleeve and held out her arm, and insisted on injecting it into the veins of her hands. She struggled to keep working, but told Leyla to keep Haddiyah away for a while. Leyla had given her information about complaints of abuse at Abu Ghraib prison, where Saddam had imprisoned, tortured, and killed scores of political opponents. The American military decided to take journalists to Abu Ghraib to show them that the prisoners were being treated well, and a group of reporters went on a tour.

Ann found it a strange and macabre tour. They were shown Saddam's torture rooms, the hall where prisoners were once hung from iron hooks, but they didn't get to see or talk to any of the present inmates of Abu Ghraib. The brief tour ended with a press conference with the American commander, Lieutenant Colonel Janis Karpinski, who refused outright Ann's request to meet some of the Iraqis presently held at Abu Ghraib. Ann had the name of a prisoner, the son of a maid at the Hotel Palestine who said her son was taken at night and she had heard nothing for months. Ann requested to meet this prisoner, and Lieutenant Colonel Karpinski ignored her question and took another from a reporter who asked about the food at the prison. Ann noticed her picture was taken several times after she asked her second question, and several officers asked to see her credentials when the briefing with Karpinski was over and the reporters were herded back outside.

The reporters exited from a different side of the prison than they had entered. Their bus was waiting for them, but from this side of Abu Ghraib, Ann could see hundreds of Iraqis crowded behind concertina wire. The prisoners screamed to get their attention. They held up signs on cardboard, one bearing the word "TORTURE." Ann heard one of those prisoners calling her name. It was a twelve-year-old boy she had interviewed in the killing fields of Al Hillal. He was waving madly to her. She remembered he was the son of the man operating the giant backhoe, spoke perfect English, knew all the state capitals, and held a firm belief that if he was brought to America, when he grew up he could help the American Olympic soccer team fare a little better on the world stage. The other reporters were almost all back on the military tour bus. Ann looked at the soldiers who had escorted the bus, and one motioned lazily with his M-16 toward the door. The boy behind the concertina was still calling: *Ann Ann Ann.* She turned and walked toward the boy, then ran. The marines yelled to her to halt. She knew she would be tackled, and she was: A short soldier drove her to the ground. Two other marines picked her up by the arms and carried her as if she was a cross back to the bus. They placed her firmly in a seat, and still without a word took away her tape recorder and notepads and camera. As the bus pulled away from Abu Ghraib, Ann looked back and thought she could see the boy behind the wire, but knew she was just picking out one of the hundreds still yelling.

☞ ☜

In July American troops killed Saddam's sons Uday and Qusay in the northern city of Mosul. Baghdad residents erupted with joy and celebrated in the traditional way, by firing rounds of live bullets into the air. Leyla walked around interviewing Iraqis as the bullets rained down around her, while Ann finished filing a story as Haddiyah slept on her bed at the Hotel Palestine. When Leyla returned, she filled Ann in on the local coverage and reaction: Despite the celebration, many Iraqis didn't believe Saddam's sons were really dead, for it was now a common belief that "Americans lie about all things." Later that day Ann went with Leyla, Haddiyah, and a CBS team up to Mosul and Saddam's hometown of Tikrit to visit the scene of the shootout, talk with troops involved, and interview townspeople. She met a man missing his arm who said it had been chewed off by a tiger owned by Uday, and a woman who had spent ten days in a room filled with snakes because she was heard to say that British prime minister Tony Blair was handsome.

When they got back to Baghdad that night it was clear Haddiyah wasn't feeling well. Leyla said she was teething. It was August, when temperatures hit 130 degrees. Leyla was dropped off at her apartment, and a few hours later called to say that Haddiyah had a fever; Ann advised her to stay indoors until the baby was better. The generator in Leyla's apartment worked most of the time, so they agreed it would be the coolest place for now. Ann made her promise to call if the generator died, and said she would pick Leyla and Haddiyah up and bring them back to her room. Then Ann went to the Hotel Palestine to work on the Tikrit story, and that night when Leyla didn't check in or answer her phone, Ann drove alone across Baghdad to her apartment. It was empty. She went back to the Hotel Palestine. Early the next morning the front desk told Ann that Leyla was on her way up. Ann shook as she waited for her. Leyla walked into her room and said of the baby swaddled in her arms: "She's dead." Ann held her, the baby against both their chests. Haddiyah's fever had spiked during the night, and both the generator and the phone had stopped working. Leyla had taken Haddiyah to four hospitals. They were full of casualties of the fighting and turned her away. Leyla had held and rocked Haddiyah until the baby quietly died in her arms as she sat by the roadside outside the last hospital.

In late afternoon, Ann and Leyla took the body to the local mosque to be buried, but there was no more room in the cemetery, and they were forced to take the baby's body back to the Hotel Palestine. Leyla placed the baby in a chair, lay face down on Ann's bed, and cried herself to sleep. Ann stood for a bit, then picked up the baby and spent the night with Haddiyah on her lap, all the while writing imaginary news reports in her head such as one that began with a four-line lead:

A beautiful baby named Haddiyah died today in Baghdad. There was no room at a single hospital for a sick baby. Now her lifeless body is in my lap. What the fuck fuck fuck am I doing here?

In the morning, Ann knelt in a large field behind a Baghdad mosque and dug a grave with a cement trowel. The ground was dried mud, and she had to scratch and stab for hours before the tiny hole was deep enough. She refused to let Leyla help her, so Leyla whispered and sang and rocked her baby. Haddiyah wore a summer dress Ann had bought her. Ann laid flowers she had bought on the black market on her body. The field was pocked with the makeshift graves of babies and children who had died in similar circumstances. Just when Ann and Leyla were going to pass out from the heat, two old women brought them a metal can of water. Ann scooped dirt and gently patted it down on Haddiyah's body, and Leyla wrote the baby's name on a scrap of yellow paper attached to a stick. Leyla and Ann held each other by the graveside and sobbed until an imam from the mosque made them leave because Ann wasn't wearing a headscarf. Later, the Iraqis would bulldoze this field for a new Iraqi government building paid for by the U.S. government. That night at the Hotel Palestine, Leyla lay curled in Ann's arms, and wiped her tears away with the scarf she had wrapped Haddiyah in as a baby. When not crying, Leyla tried to find consolation from knowing that she wouldn't have to raise Haddiyah "in this new Baghdad." She thanked Ann for promising to take her baby to America, and Ann surprised herself by saying almost angrily that she would have died before breaking that vow. Leyla fell asleep in Ann's arms on the bed. At dawn Ann awoke with words from the song "Long Black Veil" by Mick Jagger and the Chieftains running insane little loops in her head:

Nobody knows, nobody sees
Nobody knows, but me

For the next few days, Leyla and Ann stayed together in her room and walked now and then on the hotel roof, oblivious to the media chaos around them. One morning they woke up to the news that Baghdad had been hit by its first ever suicide car-bombing. Insurgents had attacked the United Nations headquarters, and Envoy Sergio Vieira de Mello was dead. The next day, Ann went to the bombed-out building with Leyla and then to the conference center in the Green Zone, where the U.S. military spokesman said, "We have entered a new phase in the war." Leyla went into a panic and told Ann that Malik had threatened a few weeks earlier to become a suicide bomber; she was afraid if he learned the war had caused the death of his daughter, he would act on his threat. Leyla also admitted that Malik had attacked her a few days before Haddiyah's death, claiming he knew Leyla was a lesbian and in love with Ann. He was high at the time on heroin, clumsy, and as they fought she bit the tip of his nose off and then escaped. She showed Ann the tip of his nose in a napkin taken from her pocket. It looked a dried blackberry. "If he doesn't blow up the Americans," Leyla said, "Malik will soon come and try to kill me, or both of us."

A few weeks later, Ann and Leyla raced to the Baghdad Convention Center and made it just in time for Ambassador Paul Bremer's big announcement: Saddam was in U.S. custody. Ann found she had no interest in the "biggest story of the war" and started to pursue other things, like violent assaults on women and girls locked day and night in their apartments and not going to school. But CBS made it clear they wanted Ann to cover *Saddam, Saddam, and Saddam*. Ann then tried to cover the growing persecution of Iraq's remaining Christians. CBS was even less interested in this. She reported on it anyway, spent time at a local church, went to the homes of some of its members. She donated Haddiyah's clothes, which Leyla had asked her to keep, to families with small children. Ann kept back a small, colorful towel Haddiyah used to love; Ann used to play peekaboo with it, and Haddiyah had thought she was hilarious.

Four Blackwater security contractors were ambushed, murdered, and hung off of a bridge in Fallujah. U.S. troops began fighting Sunni insurgents in the western city of Fallujah and fundamentalist Shiite followers of the hard-line cleric Muqtada al-Sadr in the southern city of Najaf. Civilian deaths climbed into the hundreds. Ann was told to report on the anniversary of 9/11, to go ask some troops in the street: *Does this day remind you why you are fighting here in Iraq?* Only a few soldiers she talked to believed there was a link between Saddam and 9/11: They reminded her there were no chemical weapons. Her editor wasn't happy when she filed her report. She was ordered to go to Sadr City, a slum with two million Shiites, and report on the mood toward the Americans. She and Leyla ended up surrounded by dozens of men who were furious she walked their streets in a button-down shirt and that Leyla was not wearing a hijab, and the two had to retreat to a barber shop; while the mob grew, their driver saved their lives by appealing to local elders. After that, Leyla started to wear a hijab when they went to report, although she hated it, as she loved her jeans and especially had loved wearing some of Ann's expensive shirts.

On New Year's Eve Ann and Leyla were awakened by a vicious explosion and the sounds of shattering glass. A mortar had hit a small hotel occupied by Jordanian businessmen and foreign security consultants. There were body parts everywhere. Ann was walking over human bones, flesh and blood. Later that day, CBS offered to fly her back to the U.S. for a break. Then they ordered her out. Some of her colleagues had told them Ann was having a breakdown. Ann said no. That same night, a car bomb blew up one of Baghdad's most popular restaurants, filled with a large number of foreigners. Ann knew that a group of reporter friends, including Angus, might have been there. She tried to reach him but couldn't get through, and raced to the scene to stumble through the rubble until she was grabbed by MPs and told to go back to her hotel and wait for news. Leyla came to give her the news, and Ann collapsed to the floor. Leyla somehow got Ann into the bed and rocked her. Ann sobbed into Haddiyah's scarf, then went in the bathroom and vomited and dry-heaved and screamed on and off for hours: *Alexander why? Alexander why?* She banged her skull on the floor so hard that Leyla had to trap her head in her lap. When reporters came to the door to check on Ann, Leyla talked to them in a whisper and said Ann was grieving for a dead husband and a lost baby. The reporters looked confused, but Leyla just shut the door. When Ann finally lay quietly, her green eyes open but vacant, Leyla somehow carried her to the bed, undressed her, and let her suck on her breast until she fell asleep. Two days later, Leyla told her it was her husband Malik who had blown himself up at the restaurant.

British security guards received intelligence that the Hotel Palestine was going to be attacked next. There was a lot of talk about whether the insurgents could pay the Iraqi security guards enough to betray the security around the hotel. The reporters for CNN and MSNBC had already moved to the Al Mansour, across the Tigris near the Green Zone. Then CBS moved to the Al Mansour, and Ann was told she wasn't allowed to make the move, but that a convoy of SUVs would take her to Amman. Ann said she would go to Amman, but only with Leyla. Otherwise, the two of them would simply stay at the Hotel Palestine as it emptied out and await their fates.

For a few days there was no word from CBS. The Hotel Palestine was almost deserted. Ann and Leyla left only to get food, and only with an armed guard. It was suddenly as dangerous for Leyla as it was for a Western reporter. Interpreters were starting to be abducted and murdered by the insurgents as traitors. And then one day as they were leaving the Hotel one of the Iraqi guards called out, "Ann Prendergast?" Then he waggled his tongue and said, "American girl likes Iraqi pussy?" Leyla turned and looked at Ann. Ann knew now it was truly time to leave Iraq, but still would not go without Leyla. That night two CBS reporters showed up and said they were going to Dubai and were willing to try to sneak Leyla across the border. They cut four large boxes for cameras so Leyla could lie curled within. At the border the Iraqi guards—despite a large bribe—ordered them to empty everything out. Leyla was dragged away, and when Ann ran yelling after her the Iraqi guards lowered their rifles at her. The reporters grabbed her by the arms and pulled her back to the SUV. She cursed and smashed her fist on the roof for an hour as they drove from the border, until she became aware of her fury and was quieted by the thought that she had never been so angry in her life, never felt so close to wanting to kill someone, never felt so scared by the violence hidden within her. She had no idea such uncompromising rage was possible in the diplomat's wife she knew as Ann Prendergast. It was hours later that she suddenly became aware of the texture of the seats, the cool air-conditioned glass of the window under her hand. Her hand? She admired her hand, and suddenly it was lovely. And it just *was*. Her *hand*. She covered her face with both her beautiful hands and breathed in and out. *Her* breath. *Her* lungs. The grinding sounds of the tires. Just in case Leyla was sent back, Ann had insisted that she tape to her body what money she had left, before she got in the camera boxes.

In Dubai, Ann was on the satellite phone to Baghdad all day seeking news about Leyla, at night she wandered the Sheraton like a ghost. The flash of peace or whatever it was with her hands in the SUV was forgotten. She had no money, and the satellite phone only worked because CBS hadn't turned off the account. When the two reporters left for the States, she got drunk with Japanese businessmen in their rooms and slept for a week with a British military contractor and former commando named Stephen and then for a week with an Italian businessman named Stefano, and then the three of them stayed together in one room. As she called all over Baghdad, Ann received news about two more journalists she knew who had been killed. Ann tried for new credentials from every news organization she could think of, and was told the word was out she was a whack job who had lied her way into the job.

When CBS turned off her account, Ann used Stefano's phone and tracked down a former bodyguard she knew, an ex-SAS commando who had flirted with her. He agreed to go to Leyla's apartment. He called back hours later and said Leyla didn't live there anymore and it had been taken over by Shiite militiamen. Ann heard nothing for another week. She was now with an oilman from Louisiana. Then the clerk at the front desk handed her an e-mail via the CBS bureau in

Baghdad at the Hotel Al Mansour. The subject was "Malik needs to talk to Prendergast," and it included a cell phone number. Malik was dead so it made no sense. Ann called immediately, and Leyla answered. They both cried across the hundred-mile divide, and as Ann talked on the phone she found herself sucking on a knuckle, then kissing her own hand over and over.

Leyla said it was the last time she could speak on this number; she was to begin working as an interpreter for the American military on the Fourth of July. When the Iraqis had taken her away, they were stopped by an American patrol. Leyla yelled in English that she was a translator for CBS being taken off to be raped. She jumped from the car and stood with the American soldiers, who trained their guns on the Iraqis and took her back to base, and that was how she got hired. She said she would write as soon as she had access to the army's mail service.

The next day Ann received a letter in Dubai. Leyla was living at Camp Liberty, a base at the Baghdad airport, and working with the 101st Airborne. Leyla had access to the Internet and soon sent her first e-mail, one of hundreds that Ann was to receive. She began to parse out an astounding chronicle of life on the front lines: vivid accounts of combat, the scope of the insurgency, civilian deaths, and witnessing her friends and colleagues die. Since she had no remaining close relatives, the base became Leyla's home, the American soldiers her second family. She had two marriage proposals, one from a eighteen-year-old soldier from Hawaii who she said looked like George Clooney. But what mattered most to Leyla was her new job. There were only three female interpreters on the base, and, as a result, the troops relied on her when they needed to question women civilians or prisoners. Leyla was also working with soldiers patrolling the streets of Baghdad and manning checkpoints. Though U.S. servicewomen were barred from the infantry, special operations forces, and heavy artillery units, Iraqi women were not, and Leyla was sent with American soldiers on daily missions.

One day she accompanied a squad on a mission to track down insurgents who had attacked a joint U.S.-Iraqi checkpoint with rockets, killing several American troops. On the way back one of the troops—the George Clooney look-alike—shot dead a nine-year-old Iraqi boy who had approached and offered a gift, which the soldiers thought was a bomb. Afterward, one of the soldiers opened the box and found a white mouse. When they got back to base, Leyla went to check in on the young soldier who had shot the boy. As she approached the barracks she heard a pistol shot and the soldier screaming. He had shot himself in the head but was alive, but then died in a spasm at her feet. Leyla quickly took the pistol, pointed it at herself, and pulled the trigger as other soldiers ran in. There had been only one bullet in the chamber. The soldiers initially thought she had shot him, and wrestled her to the ground, breaking her scapula. She wrote to Ann, "I have broken my angel wing," as that was what the army doctor had called it.

Leyla was admitted to the Combat Support Hospital, CASH, inside the Green Zone, normally restricted to U.S. troops. After medication and therapy for severe post-traumatic stress disorder and when her "angel wing" was healed, she was sent back to work and told that if she hung tough she would someday get a passport and a ride on a C-130 to America. She sent heart-wrenching descriptions of the black hole into which she had fallen. She was soon diagnosed with bleeding ulcers. The two other female interpreters were abducted, tortured, and killed when they left the base to return home. Their naked, headless bodies were left in the back of a Nissan truck near the base, to be discovered when the soldiers went on daily patrols. The heads were strapped into the driver and passenger seats, and shit was smeared on their faces. Leyla's letters to Ann became more alarming then, and even more so after the start of the Muslim holy month of Ramadan, when the other GI who had asked to marry her was blown up by a roadside bomb and she watched his legless torso bleed to death. She wrote of the infiltration of the Iraqi army by insurgents and terrorists. She spotted one Sunni she had seen casing the Hotel Palestine in their final days there. He saw her and saw she knew him, and he ran his finger across his throat. She ran and told a major, a search was instigated, but the Iraqi was never found.

Then days went by with no news from Leyla, and Ann panicked.

She called the number she had been given on the base and spoke with a Captain Maldrone. He told her there had been a tightening of security, and as locals, Iraqi interpreters were no longer allowed to use cell phones or the Internet, and their movements on the base were more restricted. He told Ann that if Leyla wanted to help her case, and maybe get a golden ticket to America when the Iraqi show was over, she should convert to Christianity. Ann realized Leyla was going to be cut off from her. The captain called Leyla to the phone, and Ann choked back tears as she said good-bye, knowing it would be the last time she would hear Leyla's voice for a long time. Ann soon received a letter explaining that the military now didn't trust the interpreters and searched their tents daily. Leyla added that she didn't trust her fellow interpreters either and feared they would take her money and possessions. One day, out of the blue, Ann received word that Leyla had converted to Christianity. Soon after, three male interpreters attacked Leyla in the shower house, angry that she had converted and suspicious of her motives. They banged her head on the concrete floor, and she lost consciousness, but managed to escape rape and probable death due to a fourth interpreter named Ahmed, who rushed in screaming and swinging a length of heavy electrical wire.

Ann knew it was past time to get Leyla out, if she was going to survive. But when Ann looked into it, she found that Leyla would have to flee to another country and become a refugee there before she could have a chance at resettlement. The only way she could get a U.S. visa was through a job offer, which was nearly impossible, or by marrying an American, but both of her future husbands were already dead, and Leyla had entered a dark place, was heavily medicated, and barely functioning as an interpreter.

Ann borrowed money from her family in North Carolina and took an apartment in Dubai, and she made it her full-time job to get Leyla out of Iraq. She made hundreds of phone calls and learned there were thousands of Iraqis whose lives and families were now in danger because of their work for the U.S. Leyla was on a list, but there were thousands ahead of her, but the list meant nothing, because the door was closed. In the next month, when she learned there was no way out, Leyla went into a clinical and almost catatonic depression. She lay on her cot and didn't respond to commands, and was carried back to the hospital. Medications had no effect, and she went through several rounds of electroshock therapy. This got her out of bed, and soon she was forced back out on patrol. Every few weeks she was sent back for more ECT. She told Ann it was like being kicked in the head "so you forget everything, all your feeling and all your memories, and just move like robot flesh." In early 2008, the U.S. finally issued a few visas to interpreters. Ann jumped at the chance to secure one for Leyla. But it proved to be a painstaking procedure, with at least nine separate steps, even for someone who had already been vetted by the U.S. military. Leyla had to get a new passport and a letter of recommendation from a top-ranking American general. After all the forms were finally done, her application was lost during a rotation of troops; Leyla and Ann had to start at the beginning. When the multiple forms were again in meticulous order, Leyla paid her colleague and rescuer to get her a passport in Baghdad, and she submitted all the forms and was finally issued a visa after several more months.

On another 130-degree day in August 2008, Leyla left Camp Liberty thinking she would be in Dubai with Ann by evening. But she was again stopped at the border. It turned out her passport was fake. They wouldn't let her out. The interpreter who had "bought" it for her months earlier had taken the money and duped her with a bad forgery. She was taken away in a black car. An Iraqi general sat in the back with her and pushed her head into his lap. He would get her a new passport and across the border for a hundred blowjobs; she could live at his house while she completed the contract. The general took out a gun when she refused and put it to her head. Still she refused. He drove her to a Sunni neighborhood and kicked her out of the car after stripping off her hijab, taking all the money she had taped to her stomach. She was stranded in the street at dusk topless and terrified of being killed by Sunni insurgents. She found a torn and filthy hijab in a car wrecked by an old suicide bombing. She crawled under an abandoned truck and hid until nightfall. She had put a hundred dollars in each of her shoes. She took a taxi back to the base she had left just hours earlier, but without her official badges—which she had given up—was not allowed to enter. She asked the driver if he could sell her a gun so she could kill herself. She didn't have enough cash. Right then Leyla suddenly had a clear vision of Ann's face, and asked the taxi driver to take her to the home of the Iraqi general, and there she got down on her knees on his front steps and begged to be allowed to fulfill the contract he once offered. Five months later, Leyla finally walked through Dubai customs. She walked up to Ann and said, touching her rounded stomach, "It is Haddiyah. She is here because of you."

IT WAS JUST SWIMMING

Fort Walton Beach, Florida. Him, his girl Catalina. Jimbo who was like his brother. They asked the clerk at the Best Western if the water was safe . . . of course it was safe! Fort Walton Beach was a little safe haven in a dangerous world. The clerk looked way too old to have a child, but his twins were swimming right now. Would he let his own kids swim if it was some kind of acid bath? He would not! Drop the bags, let's swim!

"God-damn-yes," was all he said. He didn't pay attention to Catalina shaking her head . . . not today. It was 101 degrees out! Who wouldn't charge the ocean? The ocean was liquid salvation! God's own swimming pool! They had driven from Grand Isle, Louisiana, on their antique Harleys. It was his idea to take this safe-water vacation. Catalina was down on the trip, but she'd come around. The glass is always half full of *water*! All he wanted to do was torpedo through the blue. He should have been a dolphin! Catalina loved that he laughed like a dolphin, a strange head-back cackle. Once he started laughing it was unstoppable. He had a birthmark on his bald dome that marked his blowhole. Right now his dome was hot as his muffler. A few hours earlier at a gas station in Pensacola he had cracked an egg to see if it would fry up there. A little girl in the car at the pump next over asked if the yolk-stain on his T-shirt was a "flutter-bye" . . . got to love that! The Big C-girl was six months pregnant, and the plan was to give birth in a Jacuzzi. He had seen videos of babies snorkeling right out of the womb, and their kid was going to be a water-baby, baby!

The clerk's twin kids were catching minnows by dragging a striped towel through the water. People up and down the beach were baking under a sherbet of umbrellas. The American flag was snapping. The sky was plutonium blue. He was going to ask his girl to marry him tonight. He'd gotten weird in the last few months, but a ring would fix all that! This was the Big Night! The zirconium ring in a boxing glove in the case of his Harley. Jimbo and him were amateur MMA heavyweight fighters. Two rabid bears in the ring. He raced his fingertips like little powerboats through the water. It pleased him still! Catalina called him Orca-man, back in their old lusty days.

There were silver minnows nibbling at his toes.

"Yo, bro!" Jimbo tackled him. All-Conference tackle for LSU. Drove him to the bottom. His bad shoulder pronged into the sand. Jimbo broke it once showing him an aikido move. He swallowed a mouthful of sand. It tasted like Clorox. A hand vised on his bicep ripped him to the surface. He corkscrewed around and forced Jimbo to dance like a marionette through the waves. Then he pressed his thumbs to his burning eyes.

"You got something on your face," Jimbo said. And there it was: just something on his face. Sand? No. Seaweed? No.

Something grainy. A weird alien stuff. He scraped his cheeks and studied orange wax under his fingernails. Nothing he loved more than swimming in the big blue. Ever since he was a kid on Grand Isle, when he got in the ocean he clapped his hands and spun around in a circle with a maniacal grin on his face. It was just something he did! Like the way a dog spins three times before settling down, the thing with water was bred in the bones of this Louisiana boy.

Once he had to spend three months in Colorado. He wanted to hang himself. He was depressed by all the *earth, earth, earth*. Friends dragged him to a turquoise lake with canyon walls, a waterfall, and a hanging garden. He wanted water? Here was some sacred water! The name of this Shangri-La? Hanging Lake. He flew home the next day. Massive chills and a fever on the plane. He passed time squeezing a plastic bottle of water, blinking at the dissected earth below. It was like he had the DTs. After landing, he took his trawler straight out into the Gulf. Stripped down, dove in, floated crucified. His chest breathed with the waves, his ribs held up the sky! When the sunset murdered the sky, he climbed back on his trawler and wept on the deck.

"To the sandbar!" And Jimbo dove under and emerged sixty feet out. It was shallow out there. On the other side of the sandbar a vigorous break. He and Jimbo bodysurfed the afternoon, their massive torsos thrown by careening, dominating waves. He rode with his arms out like skids, his broken-nosed face to the heavens, lopsided mouth grinning. A magnificent wave Mack-trucked into him and Jimbo both, and they tumbled violently across the seafloor. Catalina waved from shore.

The two stumbled over the sandbar, sore to the bones. Nothing better than total destruction by the sea gods. It tore the bullshit off you! You felt born again! Insignificant, but *alive!* He tossed an arm around Jimbo, then stopped in his tracks. Jimbo stumbled on past the grandmother at the shoreline. She lay in an aluminum lawn chair as if she had fallen from a plane, the chair half-sunk in the sand. The waves rolled their froth into her lap. It was very odd. She was shriveled to bones, and her blue housedress was sopped. He thought she was crying . . . she was crying . . . with joy. A wave suddenly toppled her over. She was on her back, waving her mottled arms in the swirling sand, like she was trying to make a sand angel! Her wig floated away like a black anemone. She was bald. He scooped her up. She clawed her fingers into his chest hair and said, "Take me out there." He looked back to the breakers, and there were two real surfers out there now. The beach was pretty empty. Catalina was watching with her hands on her hips. She looked angry.

Jimbo was already up at the showers.

So he carried someone's grandmother out to the sandbar. He walked with her in his big arms into the smashing waves. It was something he had to do. He cradled her body as the waves walloped them. She was in a cave of his strength. He had never been defeated as an MMA fighter.

A surfer railed past them, cutting and spraying. Knocked to his knees once, he held her tight in the elevator of crashing water, only to rise again from the foam like Poseidon. Coughing, choking, and gasping, she kissed his lips hard when he returned her safely to shore, even slipped him some ancient tongue. Kinky as it might seem, it was his sexiest kiss ever, although he had no idea why.

Catalina raged at the strange orange beads.

It looked like suntan lotion. The stuff was shellacked to him and Jimbo. They took turns in the outdoor shower with a bristly brush. Soap. Shampoo. Handfuls of rough sand. The water was near boiling and wafted of chlorine. The only way to get the waxy orange off was to go at it with plastic knives from the dining room of the Best Western. Even then, a couple of layers of skin were lost in the scraping!

A cloud went over the sun as he scraped at his biceps. It was the only one in the sky. He bent his neck back and laughed. Ever since he was a kid he loved to look at clouds! How many times had he almost driven his Harley off the road, stealing glances at a black stormy anvil of a cloud?

The hotel clerk's twins showed up with a bucket. There were a couple dozen silver minnows in the bucket, but only one alive. The rest bounced in funereal procession, jaw-down on the bottom. One kid was driving the live minnow along with a finger and saying, "come on, come on, you can do it!" The minnow rolled over like a fighter jet, slid to the bottom.

The twins said they were all pretty dead when they caught them in their towel. They looked at him as if to ask: Why are the minnows all dead? He gazed out to sea. He was afraid of a return of the weeping. Catalina called it that with disgust: the weeping. It was a match dropped between his legs into his Harley's open gas tank. He only wiped an eye this time, and got some of the weird alien stuff in there. It burned, and he had to squeeze the eye shut. One of the kids tossed the bucket on the sand. The dead minnows clutched at the sunset, angry red exclamation marks in the sand. When he was a boy on Grand Isle, they'd catch hundreds of minnows with a towel. As long as they kept them cool under a porch and changed the seawater every few hours, they'd live until they could be slipped onto a fishhook and dropped off the back of his father's shrimper when the nets were up. They didn't just *die*.

The twins settled down to build a castle in the wet sand from the shower. One of the boys had gold braces on his teeth, the other's mouth a rainbow. As a boy he used to build moats around his castles by the beach showers in Grand Isle while waiting for his father to dock the trawler. He came from two centuries of shrimpers. Acadian men, only alive at sea. Now *Frere Jacques* was on cinderblocks. Too much of the fiberglass of the hull dissolved! The shrimp were now black and sometimes mutated. His father collected two-headed shrimp, kept them in beer bottles in rubbing alcohol.

His shower water raced down the newly carved river toward the castle of the twins, but evaporated on the journey to their moat. The boys glumly surveyed the failed flow. Their castle was a half-assed pile with slapped handprints. It looked like there were streaks of oil in the sand.

He shoved his face directly under the showerhead, and decided to teach them how to make a castle with towers and turrets as soon as the weird stuff was off his skin. He never understood why adults wanted to rinse the sea salt off. Skin burned and crisped, salted and cooled by the evening stars of a beach, was the only tuxedo for him! He wouldn't be in the shower now except for the caul of freaky orange stuff on his skin. The night he had originally planned: him in a salt tux with mahi-mahi and daiquiris and karaoke, walks on the beach with champagne in fluted glasses the shape of his Catalina (even with the baby!), a midnight bridal carry into the sea under the full moon and a diamond ring sparkling in the sunrise.

He was blinking one eye like an insane pirate, and said to the boys, "Arrgh, I'm a pirate now, mateys! Will ye join my ship?"

One kid said his throat was burning. The boy was gripping his neck. "It really hurts!" Jimbo bought both kids Cokes and told them to gargle it.

"Where's my mother?"

"Isn't your father the clerk of the hotel?"

The boys gazed at him as if he was dangerous. He turned and jogged into the Best Western. The new desk clerk reported that Gil had no children, but liked to mess with the heads of guests.

"We'll find your mother. Don't worry buddy," he said when he returned to the beach. He took the stricken boy by the hand. He felt strange. Discombobulated. His skin itched. Maybe it was the fierce rubbing with the bristly brush. His arms and chest were blotchy. His eyelid was sealing itself shut. Where was the kid's mother? Jimbo had the other kid by the hand and was telling him to keep gargling. Jimbo had a strange faith in the curative power of Coke.

The mother was Cuban and a hundred yards down the beach. Her bathing suit looked like a pink tutu. She was screaming at him and Jimbo in Spanish. Why were these giant tattooed men—one with a spastic eye—holding her little boys by the hand and dragging them down the beach? Both kids were now freaked as well as sick. The boy with the sore throat was bent over and gagging, and the other boy was hyperventilating.

A crowd was gathering. The beach had been nearly empty, now there was a circle of hostile Cuban-looking men. Why didn't the mother get it? The boy was sick! The woman should listen to him, damn it! He put on his command voice from the navy. He had been a chief petty officer, a trained deep-sea diver. He had gone down two thousand feet in a diving bell, where a mistake crushed you like a beer can under a semi.

"We were worried about your boy, we're not pervs. Jimbo got him a Coke. Look at his face. He's chalk white. He should be burned, or red, after a day in this sun. And he's freezing—he's got chills. Go to Fort Walton Beach Hospital! Do not pass go! *Tu comprendes doctore? Ir al medico!* Look at the other boy. He looks like he's going down too. Listen, let's help you get them to your car. The kid's legs are wobbling. Can you keep up, ma'am?" The beach was strangely spinning now.

Catalina was pointing to the specks of orange goo on the kid's mullet and calling 911. Kid number two was in some sort of asthma attack. He lay on his back waving his arms and legs like a poisoned cockroach. His face was gray, his pupils like dinghies in a storm. Black spittle was bad, pretty freakish. The mother didn't speak English but was on her knees slapping her palms and wailing for *Jesus*. The Cuban men were no longer threatening, but in a circle encouraging him to save the boys, as if they might choose not to!

He scooped up the boy who was clawing the air. The beach was spinning under him, but he charged with the boy to his Harley. Taking action! The boy had his eyes locked on him. He knew that look, had seen it on divers with the bends: Please don't let me die! He had trained as a medic in the navy, and carried a first-aid kit, including Epi-pen, on his Harley. He gently laid the gasping kid on the broken sidewalk and jabbed him with the epinephrine. Jimbo had gathered up the other boy and was standing right behind him. He heard the boy vomiting, the warm bile spraying his back. It didn't bother him. He'd put his life on the line a dozen times to save drowning sailors. Once, he dove off an aircraft carrier at night to rescue a suicidal sailor. The admiral asked him later how he found the sailor in the black water. He said in the ocean, a sort of weird primordial GPS took over his body.

The mother in the pink tutu was again praying over her son. He had to push her out of the way to check the boy's pupils. He pushed her too hard, and she tumbled under his Harley. There was a crowd now: the Cuban men, and rubberneckers climbing out of stopped cars. A drunken woman kept accidentally banging him with her knee as she touched the boy's cheek and told him it would be allllright, help is on the way. Traffic backed up and honking. There was no ambulance and fixed pupils.

He scooped the boy, motioned to Catalina with his chin. She jumped on his Harley and kicked it over, and he got on behind her with the boy in his arms. Jimbo handed the other boy to a short man in a tank top that said *Havana Is for Lovers*, jumped on his Harley, and the man climbed on with the boy. The tutu-ed mother scrambled onto the back of Jimbo's bike, and he slid his crotch up over his gas tank.

Catalina roared down the middle turning lane of a five-lane road. Near Benny's Pawn Shop they were almost sideswiped by a FedEx truck. A cop pulled behind them, siren wailing. By speaker the cop said to pull over, then pulled alongside. Jimbo yelled over that they had two dying kids. The cop pulled ahead of them, and soon they were blowing down the road at seventy, busting through intersections with barely a slowdown. His kid still wasn't breathing, but they were at the hospital!

He and Jimbo charged with the kids. No nurses at the admitting desk, so he elbowed a security guard and smashed into the ER. That got their attention! Bells and whistles and sirens! Nurses, doctors, security out of the woodwork. The Cuban mother was doing her hysterical thing. The cop was with her. The kids were tossed on two gurneys, and Code Blue was in full force. The security guards shoved him and Jimbo out the double doors, and then told the cop to clear the crazy bikers from the waiting room.

A doctor with a handlebar mustache was asking what he knew . . . what he knew? He knew those twin kids were just playing on Fort Walton Beach! Building a sandcastle like every other American kid in summer! That's not supposed to be playing with napalm! There was something in the water! In the water! The minnows were all belly-up. That was a sign like in the Bible! Not as good as frogs from the sky, but still! No, he wanted to be more help, *he did!* But he was a shrimper, not a doctor: He knew the minds of blue crabs and shrimp, the moods of kingfishers and laughing gulls and spoonbills, the salt of Barataria Bay from the brackish tang of the inlets and estuaries and marshes. He knew how to catch croaking male redfish with mud-minnows, his mother and father's gumbo secrets, diesel engines, his friend Jimbo, but most of all, he knew Catalina here! He knew her tides and moons and sudden sunrises and had since they were in fifth grade—so he knew things, but he didn't know why the water in the ocean was killing those kids. But why didn't the doctor take his thumb out of his ass and save those kids? How about *now!*

The doctor's gray eyebrows flew up just as Jimbo fell like a snapped mast. His linebacker's body dropped back to the red and green linoleum floor. Catalina tried to catch him. Jimbo's eyes were wide open as if he had seen a UFO. The doctor had his fingers on Jimbo's thick neck. Catalina had tumbled hard, and was sitting with her arms nestled around her pregnant belly. The doctor had his ear to Jimbo's mouth watching his chest, and yelled he's not breathing! Nurses tore open Jimbo's shirt as they lifted him onto a gurney. There was the chest with the missing nipple from the shrimp-truck wreck in Morgan City when he was seventeen.

Catalina cried out her water had broken. Her yellow sarong sopped between her legs. She was lifted onto a gurney and driven like a wedge through the double doors. Catalina yelled we want a water birth! He was holding Catalina's hand and repeating It's OK, baby, it's OK. But it wasn't OK. She was hysterical about the water birth. Jimbo was riding on a gurney behind them with his own posse of doctors and nurses. They parked Jimbo in one stall, Catalina in the other. Between them was a hanging sheet covered in gaudy tropical fish. Catalina's sarong was tossed aside, and her legs scissored open and there was a crescent of wet, bloody skull. Catalina's upper molars sparkled as she gasped she wanted a water birth. The doctor was saying, *Bear down now!*

He poked his head around the sheet. Jimbo was naked and blue. There was a breathing tube down his nose. Handlebar Doctor was working compressions like he worked the winch on his trawler. They zapped Jimbo's heart with the paddles. Handlebar Doctor glared up at the red numbers of the digital clock and stopped compressions. *Handlebar stopped compressions!* He flipped the curtain back and moved to his friend's side. He continued compressions and called out to Jimbo. He'd saved at least five lives in the navy with CPR. Sometimes he compressed so hard he broke ribs, *but they lived!* Handlebar put a hand on his bicep. There was a gooey white stuff bubbling out of Jimbo's mouth. It looked like yogurt. He wiped it off his chin. The nurses were filing out. Jimbo looked like he had been punched in both eyes. He kept pumping on his chest. He hit his chest with his fist and screamed: *Jimbo, man, fuck no!* Security circled, and the cop, but the doc pushed them back and pulled the screen around. Jimbo's pupils were black opals.

There wasn't any noise coming from the stall next to Jimbo's. He kissed his Jimbo on the forehead and ducked around the fish curtain. Catalina was curled on her side. A nurse was stroking her blond hair. She was explaining they had to get the afterbirth. The doctor was mouthing the words I'm sorry. A nurse was holding the baby, his skin translucent like a shrimp. He tried to hold Catalina's hand, but she squeezed his fingers backwards violently. She was trying to break his fingers. She swiveled her head and whispered, "God damn your ocean." He was going to let her break his fingers, but she let go. The nurse holding their son asked if he'd like to hold him. He took the baby in his big arms, and for a split-second saw the *Frere Jacques'* motor across his blue eyes. He moved his lips as if they belonged to someone else. "You were going to be a trawler-man. A seventh-generation Louisiana shrimper."

A nurse with a face like a lobster took the baby away. The itchiness started on his arms. He scratched and looked down. His arms were covered in sores, horrible lipstick lesions the size of a dime. They looked like the bites of a brown recluse. He pulled his T-shirt up, and his hairy chest and gut were covered in the same nasty red sores. There was white pus coming from them as if they were giant zits. He scratched at them, and a few burst. The pus burned on his fingers, and where it dribbled on his body new red sores broke out. The nurses were looking him like he was being taken over by aliens. There was a conversation outside the fish curtain. Handlebar Doctor glanced at his chest and arms and face. The sores were now breaking out on his face. He must have gotten the pus on his face with his fingers. A nurse, the cop, and four orderlies dragged him from the bedside of Catalina and their baby. Down a hall and through double steel doors into a quiet baby-blue room. There was a huge stuffed giraffe in the corner. The nurse came back in wearing a plastic bodysuit, a face mask, and gloves, like he had anthrax. Now the sores were all over his legs and ass. He could not sit down or lie down, and she cut his clothes off with giant steel scissors.

The nurse was dabbing wildly at his sores with Epsom-salt solution. Every time she broke one, two more popped out. Then she dropped a cotton ball and ran from the room. He looked in the mirror. He no longer had a neck. His face was a featureless skin bag covered with oozing sores like the pox. His whole body was now in flames. It was as if he was dipped in a pool of molten lead. He could see the cover of a book Catalina used to read to his nephews: *Alexander and the Terrible, Horrible, No Good, Very Bad Day.* The doctors were swarming him now, and he was gasping spasmodically as his throat swelled. He was flat on the hospital bed now, and they were jamming a plastic tube into his mouth. It didn't work so they gave him a tracheotomy. He was breathing now from a hole in his throat. They were all masked, but he could see Handlebar Doctor. They took blood samples. A doctor raced back in and said, "He's lit up with bacteria like a Christmas tree."

He started to gag. His baby was dead. His friend was dead. His girl was dead to him. Bile was climbing out of his blocked throat. He heard Handlebar Doctor say I've shot him with enough Prednisone to kill a horse. He was gagging up black bile now. He was bent over the side of the bed and puked on the floor. There were hunks of crud in his puke like asphalt raisins. He had no idea how much time had passed. A doctor ran in, a specialist, who said it looked like mycoplasma pneumonia. Then he left! An allergist came in and glanced at his sores and said they looked like scabies, and then he left too! He heard the allergist yelling in the hall how he wasn't going to get called into court for the next twenty years! A screwdriver of a headache hit him, and he started to shiver so badly his jaw was clacking open and shut.

Glands were swollen all over his body. It was like the plague. The swellings in his groin were the size of ping pong balls. His lungs were filled with fluid. They drained them with a big needle. He breathing was labored, and he started to sweat. It was like every pore in his body was leaking at once. But he had no temperature! You can't sweat buckets without a spike in temp! He was coming back negative negative negative on all the tests. He saw another needle, and they popped him with the biggest antibacterial shot you can get . . . and then the biggest dose of viral antibiotic! But he was still sweating like a marathoner in the Mojave. The sheets were swimming. It was like all the salt water in his body was fleeing at once. He was losing so much water they had to put in four IVs. Water was dripping out of his nose, and a new doctor said: "He has a temperature of 97.8 and is expelling water so fast he's going to be dead from dehydration in an hour even with the IVs. His white blood cells are crazily low and his red cell count is crashing. This is some sort of brand-new illness. It's time to call the CDC." He heard another doctor say, "I've got four autopsies already of people who went swimming today. I've seen dissolved esophagus, enlarged hearts, and we've got samples of ethylbenzene, M2P-xylene, hexane-2, methylpetane, and isooctane in their blood." And later Handlebar Doc said, "This guy's body is full of things you wouldn't believe. He's got a negative-style bacterium, and the only match I can find is a microbe that eats oil."

He raised his head to look down at his naked body strapped to the hospital bed, and he was *totally gray, like a zombie!* And what was oozing from all his dozens of sores was nothing he'd call blood, it was dark, maybe black . . . his hands were now waving spastically, and he was calling in his mind: *Catalina! Catalina!* He clobbered two nurses, and they got orderlies and strapped his arms and legs to the bed and juiced him in both arms with happy drugs. He was flying over ten or eleven shrimp trawlers. There was a rendezvous off Grand Isle at the solstice sunset. They had rafted their trawlers together. Their outrigger booms were all up as if in surrender. He came out of his cabin and shot off his gun a few times directly at the sunset, drank two beers, and collapsed on the aft deck. He smoked some pot and the nausea retreated, and then he took visitors as they clambered over the side to take his limp hand. A lot of these guys had been his sworn enemies. Jesus! They were going to miss him! They were terrified for themselves and the shrimp and their families too, scared of what got him, what was in the water. He saw the new look on their faces as they watched their kids leaping off his cockpit into the Gulf of Mexico. His son would have jumped, too, in five years! He stumbled below with his gun and dragged out the clerk from the Best Western, the one who said it was safe to swim. He ordered one of the outrigger booms lowered, and pulled a line tight around the clerk's neck. He pointed to his father to throw the switch, and with a hydraulic grind the boom rose slowly, the clerk kicking a few last times over the now tranquil sea.

CPSIA information can be obtained at www.ICGtesting.com
Printed in the USA
BVOW05s0247150915

417668BV00007B/19/P